Chase

Lysa Walker

Runaway Publications

lysawalker@runawaypublications.com
http://www.runawaypublications.com

ISBN: 978-1-304-97578-2
Publisher: Runaway Publications
Rights Owner: Lysa Walker

CHASE

"You can't make him pay for his sins. Chase has no fear. He doesn't love anything or anyone, not even himself. I know what he's capable of. You can't underestimate him. The only way to beat him is to be even more heartless than he is and to do that means you can't have anything to lose yourself."

"Trisha, you talk about him like nobody can get to him. He's always out in the open. He's a easy target."

"If you think that then what's stopping you? What happens if you miss? What do you think he'll do to you?"

"I've seen him hurt too many people Trisha including people I love."

"You helped him hurt a lot of those people. So who's going to judge you?"

"I know what I've done but your nephew is a monster Trisha. He's heartless and you never know what he's going to do. I can't be a part of that anymore."

"I remember having this same conversation a long time ago, about my sister Sasha. Sasha was the one that killed Chase's mother, right in front of him."

"Your sister Sasha? I thought Chase's mother was your sister."

"She was; Kisha was the oldest. Sasha blamed Kisha for the death of our mother and she spent most of her life hating Kisha and wanting revenge but she wanted to watch Kisha suffer first. Right before she killed Kisha she pointed a gun at Chase, he was Chase Jr. at the time. He was only five years old. I wasn't going to let that happen."

"So you were there?"

"Yea, I stopped her from shooting Chase Jr. but I couldn't stop her from shooting Kisha. After that is when things got worse."

"Shit. How much worse could it get?"

"I should have just grabbed Chase and left but I didn't. I made stupid choices. Chase's hate for Sasha built up the same way Sasha's hate built up for Kisha. When Chase turned fifteen he killed Sasha. The same way his mother was killed and with the same exact rage."

“Trisha?’

“Yea.”

“Did you hear that? “

CHASE
CHAPTER ONE

"Spazz grab that motherfucker before he gets in the car and bring him back in the house! Fresh you and Chino take the cars and block off the streets on each end, nobody gets through!"

"What about the cops Chase?"

I didn't answer Chino, by now he should know the answer to that. Fresh grabbed Chino pushing him in the direction of the cars. I could still hear this chick screaming from the second floor. I waited for Spazz who was dragging Brick up the stairs. I looked at both ends of the block to make sure my boys had it covered then I ran back upstairs.

"Sit him down!" I stood in front of the chairs.

Spazz pushed Brick down in the chair right next to his wife. Ant stood behind her to make sure she remained calm. At the moment he wasn't doing a good job of it.

"Brick he's going to kill us!" Brick's wife was screaming.

"Yes I am." There was no reason to lie to her.

"Chase I swear to God man, I don't have it."

"Brick I swear to God man! I don't believe you."

Ant laughed at me.

"I was on Prince Street. This dude walked past me then stopped and lit his cigarette. I ain't think nothing of it. I turned my head for a second to look up the street and when I turned back he had a gun in my face. I didn't have to tell him where my stash was, he already knew."

"What did this dude look like?" Ant asked walking around Brick and standing directly in front of him.

"I don't know Ant, I never seen him before. That's my word; I'll put that on my life."

"You just did my friend." Ant put his hand on Brick's shoulder and walked away.

"Do you know it's in a person's nature to lie when they're afraid?" I asked him.

"Chase please listen to me. I'm not lying! I would never steal from you. Never! Don't do this!"

"Brick, understand my position. Product and money is missing. Product that you're responsible for and this isn't the first time. Ant saved you last time but it's not looking good for you today so either you got my money or you got my product."

"I don't have it! I didn't steal from you, I swear to God!"

"You swearing to God does nothing for me."

"Listen to me; I'm here. You got me. Let my wife go. She don't have shit to do with this!"

"I can't do that." I walked away.

We watched them huddle up and pray to God for forgiveness of their sins and to watch over their kids after they were gone.

"Tie him up Spazz."

The wife started screaming again when Spazz pulled them apart.

"Chase think about this. You're going to regret this!" Brick was reaching for his wife.

"Regrets are for people who are not sure about the decisions they make Brick." I nodded at Spazz to hurry up.

"Chase I will get you the money back, just give me a chance to get it." Brick was desperate.

"I'll make a deal with you Brick. If you can get me the money in say the next five seconds then I'll let you and your wife go. No hard feelings. Spazz get ready to untie them."

Spazz smirked at me; Brick put his head down and stared at the floor.

"Chase you know I don't have that kind of money. I need some time."

"I'm giving you time, five seconds and I haven't even started counting yet."

"Ant, don't let him do this!" Brick was appealing to Ant but he was wasting his time.

Ant didn't even look in his direction. I nodded at Spazz who was already waiting for the next move; he ran out the apartment. Ant walked over and stood by the door.

"What about our kids? Are you that heartless?!" It was Brick's wife turn to convince me to not kill them both.

We could hear Spazz running back up the stairs; just in time. He came in with the gas can and handed it to me.

"Chase what the fuck are you about to do?" Brick was getting hysterical.

I opened the can and walked over to Brick's wife. I looked down into her eyes that were staring back at me. She quickly looked down when I emptied the gasoline over her head. She started to choke from the amount of gas that has gone in her mouth. It didn't take her long to start screaming again.

"I'm going to set your wife on fire Brick and then watch her set you on fire to."

Brick didn't speak; he just looked at his wife with tears rolling down his face. She was still coughing and screaming. Brick was trying his best to get out of the ropes.

I lit the match and tossed it. Brick's wife screamed even louder as the flames melted away her skin. At first Brick screamed for his wife but soon after he screamed from the pain. The fire spread like butter over the both of them and melted everything in its path after that. We had to move, the three of us ran out of the apartment and down the stairs. The screaming had stopped but the fire was still spreading. Fresh and Chino were outside staring at the flames coming out of the windows from the second floor. I jumped in my car with Spazz and Ant right behind me. I pulled off watching the flames from my rearview; it had completely covered the house. I dropped my boys off and went home. I was tired and smelled like smoke. I had a feeling that Wise would be waiting up for me and I was right.

"What happened?" Wise was sitting on the couch.

"With what?"

"You know with what. What happened with Brick, Chase?"

"I handled it."

"Why didn't you call me?"

"I didn't need to call you. I handled it."

"Yea, I know you could handle it. It's how you would handle it that got me worried. Where's Brick?"

"Gone."

"Gone? Chase?"

"What?"

"That shit wasn't necessary Chase!"

"Product and money is gone. It was necessary!"

"What you do?"

"A fire broke out; unfortunately Brick and his wife didn't make it out."

He was quiet for a second. We had different ways of doing things some times and he always got upset whenever I didn't agree with him. The father role that he was trying to play with me was getting old. Him helping my family in the past and his relationship with my aunt is what keeps the peace but lately we're not on the same page, the peace was ending.

"What the fuck is wrong with you Chase? I didn't ok that shit!"

"You didn't ok it? You're funny and I'm tired. We can argue about this tomorrow."

"No unnecessary deaths! That's what we agreed on, that's what I've always taught you."

"Stop talking about what you taught me! I don't want to hear that shit. I run this and the decision to end Brick's life was necessary. Point blank period!

"You don't even get it."

"What don't I get Wise?"

"It's messy Chase! What about other houses on the block? Do you know how many people probably got hurt because of that fire?"

"So what! It's done."

He turned around and walked away. As soon as he hit the doorway I heard "stupid motherfucker". Like I said it's the relationship he has with my aunt that keeps the peace. I slammed my bedroom door behind me and laid across the bed. Eventually I fell asleep.

"Chase!"

Trisha's voice woke me up. I sat up and tried to focus. She didn't wait two seconds before she started screaming again.

"Chase!"

"What!"

"Phone!"

"Who is it?"

"I don't know, answer it and find out!"

Who would be calling for me on the house phone? Nobody I know has that number and why would they call that instead of my cell phone? I grabbed my phone and looked at it. It was on and no missed calls. I got up.

"Here." She handed me the phone when I walked into the kitchen.

"Hello."

"Hello Chase."

"And you are?"

"This is Papo speaking. I've heard that you want to meet me. Today at 3pm, get the address from Chino." He hung up.

Papo was the only reason I made Chino apart of the team. Papo was Chino's pops and he also supplies most of Essex County NJ with cocaine. I want to help him supply all of NJ. My team right now is six strong. Myself, Wise, Ant, Fresh, Spazz, and Chino. They all answer to me. Wise is the only one that has somewhat of a say in how we handle business and that's because him and a couple of his friends helped me establish shit in Newark when we got out here. Wise is originally from Newark and is related to Ant; my best friend. Our families met in Atlanta and when we had to leave they came with us. Spazz and Fresh came later; they were the neighborhood trouble makers. They were always in the streets causing all kinds of shit. They robbed, car jacked and fucked with people for no reason. The neighborhood was scared but to me I saw potential. It didn't take too long for them to become part of the team. Now Chino was different. No street knowledge and no intelligence but I still put him to work. Once I found out who his father was, I knew Chino would be my way in. His job on the team was surveillance. I make him feel useful and he gets me in with his father. Wise walked in the kitchen right after I got off the phone. He kissed Trisha, walked past me and sat down at the table. He looked up at me and nodded good morning. I laughed and walked out.

"Chase!"

I kept walking. I went into the bathroom and turned the shower on. I remembered I had to call Ant and tell him to meet me tonight. I want to be out on the block tonight. If someone really is robbing my workers then I want to know who it is. I had to make an example out of Brick, I had no choice. I took a quick shower and got ready to start my day.

"Chase." Wise was standing outside the bathroom door.

"Damn! What?"

"I know you heard me calling you when you walked out the kitchen."

"Yea I heard you."

"Do we have a problem Chase?"

"You tell me Wise."

"That attitude you're wearing is not conducive to us having a productive partnership."

"Well whenever you're ready to sever the partnership and leave the team, you let me know."

"You would love that but nah, I'm good. What's on the schedule for today?" He smiled at me.

"I got a meeting with Papo at three."

"How you manage that?"

"He called me."

"Okay. I'm going over to see Muhammed and Kane today. Ask them to join the team. I think they need our help as much as we would need theirs and if we going to be getting into bigger things than it's definitely necessary."

"Just remember your team is my team and if they have problems with doing what they told to do, it's not going to work."

"Chase, relax. Muhammed and Kane been in the game for a long time way before you were even thought of."

"See, I don't need to hear all that. What I'm telling you is make sure they know that they can't do their own thing if they part of this team."

"I will handle Mu and Kane. You don't have anything to worry about. What's your problem?"

"I have a problem with you talking to me like I don't know what the fuck I'm doing."

"Before you two start arguing, knock it off!" Trisha screamed walking past us.

I went in my room and finished getting dressed. Wise bringing in Muhammed and Kane wasn't an issue for me because they're soldiers. I remembered them from back in the day. They helped us out in Atlanta and they originally were from Jersey to. Having them on the team would be beneficial but how they handle me as their boss is something I need to see. I called Chino and got his address then I called Ant and left him a message telling him I needed him tonight.

CHASE
CHAPTER TWO

"You're too young to be so cocky." Papo sounded like Wise for a minute and it was pissing me off but I had no choice but to let that ride.

"Please don't mistake my confidence for arrogance Papo. I just know what needs to be done."

"And what is that exactly?"

"Make money. Right now I only supply the streets but you supply the neighborhoods. You have to want more, I know I do. Together both our numbers increase. Chino already told me your numbers."

"My stepson talks too much sometimes."

A young girl in a school uniform walked in.

"Digame cuando termines con él. (Let me know when you're done with him.)" She kissed Papo on the Cheek.

"Segura cariño. (Will do sweetheart)"

She shook her head and gave me a dirty look before she left the room.

"Leticia!"

Papo called out to her, she rolled her eyes and kept walking. This must be Chino's little sister, you could tell she was spoiled. I laughed at her.

"Excuse my daughter Chase; she sometimes lets her emotions show when she shouldn't."

"No worries."

"What does trust mean to you Chase?" Papo looked at me seriously.

"It means nothing to me." I gave him an honest answer.

"It sounds like your answer comes from anger."

"No it comes from experience."

"What experience could you have at such a young age?"

"Experience and age don't always go hand in hand Papo. A twenty five year old could have more experience than a fifty five year old depending on how they lived their lives."

"Si (Yes)." Papo shook his head.

"I have a question for you though."

"Ask it."

"Why isn't your son a bigger part of your business?"

"He's my stepson. I love him and I will always provide for him but he is not a leader. That is why I've decided to give you a chance but first I need something done. This will prove how competent you are and if I can do business with you on a permanent basis. A stranger from Miami is out here. He is buying and reselling my product. Normally that wouldn't concern me but he is altering the quality of my product and still using my name to distribute it. I found out through some contacts that his name is Cuco; I want you to handle that for me. Here is a picture and his is information."

"Enough said, I'll take care of it."

"Bueno (Good)."

I shook Papo's hand and I got up. As I got to the door, I saw the shadow of a person walking away but I didn't care. I was feeling good about the meeting. This is what I've been waiting for, an opening. I wanted it all and I knew exactly how I was going to get it. I drove to the address on the piece of paper and parked by a bar across the street from the building. As soon as he came out of the building I knew it was him by his curly hair and the mole on his face. He jumped into a cab, what was interesting to me was the black car following the cab. Eventually I'm going to have to find out who that is but not right now; I'll have Chino check it out. When I got home I could hear Trisha and Wise talking in the kitchen.

"What's up?" I stuck my head in.

"Hey Chase." Trisha smiled at me.

"How did the meeting go with Papo?" Wise nodded at me and I walked into the kitchen.

"Good. I have to handle a small situation for him, some dude name Cuco. Somebody's following him though. I put Chino on it. We'll talk about that tonight."

"Ok cool, speaking of tonight. I need to talk to you before the meeting."

"About what?

"A situation that we need to take care of."

"Bring it to the table." I didn't even want to talk to him.

"If I wanted to bring it to the table than I wouldn't be trying to talk to you about it before the meeting."

"What's so important?"

"What's the attitude for?"

“Don’t worry about my attitude. Say what you need to say.”

“Never mind I’ll wait for the meeting.”

“I don’t have time for this shit.” I started to walk out of the kitchen.

“You’re acting like a little kid.”

“What does that mean?”

“That means grow the fuck up.”

“There are no kids in here Wise and there never was as far as you’re concerned.”

“What does that mean?”

“That means that you’re not my father.”

“No I’m not but I’m the man that raised you.”

“Raised me?! You looked out for me but don’t confuse that with raising me.”

Wise got up from the table, walked around and stood in front of me. Trisha jumped up and started to run towards us but Wise put his hand out for her to stay there.

“I was the only father you had and I did what a father was supposed to do for his son. You’re going to respect that.”

“I’m going to respect that? How you planning on making that happen? You don’t have a son here. Only one man held the title of my father and he’s dead. The only way you could compare is if you’re dead to.”

I stepped closer in his direction.

The anger came out and he used both of his hands to push me into the wall. If the wall wasn't there I would have probably hit the floor. I was able to bounce off the wall and I swung as hard as I could. Wise stumbled back and hit the floor. I knew he wasn't going to stay down for long and would jump back up with a vengeance. I was prepared, I pulled my gun out.

"No!!!!!!!!"Trisha screamed.

I put a bullet in the wall right next to his head. The sound of the gun going off didn't shock him; it was the fact that I was the one that shot at him that had him with the confused look on his face. He didn't move or speak, he just stared.

"What the hell are you doing Chase?! Are you crazy?!" Trisha was hysterical.

I slowly put the gun away and Wise got off the floor. He never once looked away.

"Stay out of it Trisha." Wise was talking to Trisha but still staring at me.

"No! I'm done with this crazy shit! I'm telling both of y'all I'm done with it!"

Trisha looked like she was about to have a nervous breakdown so I decided to leave but not before making something clear to Wise.

"Wise?"

"What?"

"I missed on purpose."

"Oh Yea?"

"Yea. I don't want you dead but if I did......." I shrugged my shoulders and continued to walk out of the kitchen.

"Chase?"

I could hear the anger in his voice. I stopped in the doorway but didn't turn around.

"You get no points for warning shots. Next time that bullet might be meant for you."

I walked out. Trisha was running behind me. This is what I was trying to avoid.

"Chase!"

I didn't stop, I started walking a little faster to get to the front door but she caught me and grabbed my arm. Pulling away from her wasn't an option, she was holding on tight. She made me turn around to face her.

"This is not going to happen Chase, not with him."

"I'm not going to kill your boyfriend Trisha."

"You're my nephew Chase and I love you. I have always been there when you needed me and that's something that you have to respect. Wise isn't your father but he's been the closet thing to one and you and I both know that. Whatever issues you got with him, end it. End it now before something bad happens. I know that tragedy is following you but it's got to stop here. I don't have the energy to go through this anymore."

"Tragedy is following me? What are you talking about?"

"Our family is gone. One by one, murdered. Gone! Tragedy is following all of us. You grew up around so much bullshit and you embraced it. There was nothing I could do to stop you but I won't let you kill another person I love. Make peace with Wise and do it now!"

"Ok." Was all I said.

I walked back towards the kitchen and stood in the doorway until Wise looked up at me. I knew he was aching to shoot back at me but I also knew that he would make peace if only for Trisha.

“We good?” I said with a smirk on my face.

“We good.” He with anger on his.

I walked out the kitchen and out of the front door.

CHASE
CHAPTER THREE

I was sitting at the table when everyone walked in. Wise and I hadn't spoke since this morning but we was about to put that shit aside to take care of business.

"Chase what's the news on Cuco?"He spoke first.

"What you find out Chino?" I looked at Chino.

"Cuco is down here from Miami. Got out of jail three months ago and been down here for about two months now. So far, once a month he takes a trip back to Miami." Chino was reading from a notebook.

"Who's following him?" I need to find out who that is.

"I don't know. I couldn't tell."

"We can't make any moves until we find out." Wise was concerned.

"How is he transporting?" Ant turned to face Chino.

"Rental car."

"How much is he taking back with him? Fresh asked the next question.

"Five keys. Papo changed the price on him to thirty six and he still got it." I was getting mad just at the thought of that.

"Sounds like he's got clientele." Spazz leaned on the table.

"That's about to end." I meant that.

"How did he know to come here for the product?" Ant was grilling Chino.

“I don’t think he knew. I think he just took a chance and lucked up.”

“No one thinks Jersey is a hot coke spot. Somebody told him to come here.” Wise made a good point.

“Right.” I nodded my head at him.

“We getting dirty on this?” Ant looked over at me.

“Absolutely.”

“Is that what Papo wants?” For some reason Wise felt the need to question everything I fucking did. I ignored his ass.

“Chino, don’t your pops have his own people to take care of shit like this?” Spazz was curious.

“Yea but his people take care of big problems. To him, Cuco is a small one.”

“Then why not just have you handle it?” Fresh asked.

“He doesn’t trust me with things like that.” Chino looked at me, I smiled at him.

“Me and Ant got this covered, no need for a group event.” I looked directly at Chino when I said that.

“Sounds good.” Ant shook my hand.

“I’m not coming? I’m the one that got all the info.” Chino was pissed.

“No, I got who I need. Next matter for the table.” I looked over at Wise and gave him the table.

“Denise Johnson, a long time friend came to me about a situation. Her twelve year old daughter was raped by two men coming home from school; behind prince street projects. She seen them before and I know who she's talking about. I want to handle that ASAP."

"Tell her to call the police Wise. That's not what we do." I couldn't believe he brought some shit like that to the table.

"It's what I do Chase."

"No that's what you use to do. Your superhero days are over. There is no money in that."

"It's not about money. It's about taking care of the people that need our help."

"Forget it. We're not getting involved with that."

"I say we are." Wise leaned in on the table and looked me straight in the eye.

"You have no say at this table."

"Says who? You? My business is what got us all out here, safe."

"Your business is over."

"There was a time when you and your family needed me and my crew. My business saved your life."

"How's that working out for you? Most of your crew is dead! And you? You had to leave Atlanta and come back to where you started from. Selling drugs under the command of a twenty five year old."

"What?" Wise felt disrespected.

"Can we get back to the matter on the table?" Ant always felt stuck in the middle.

"Your time is gone Wise. Your way of doing things in the past is over. Everybody at this table is under me and that includes you."

"I never was or will be under anybody's command." Wise banged his hand on the table.

"If you say so. Bottom line is that shit is too risky."

"Risky? We sell drugs Chase!"

"What you're talking about is risk with no financial gain."

"Chase, financial gain is not always what it's about. You can't keep taking from the streets and not give anything back. There's got to be a balance."

"Yea a balance of zero is what we're going to end up with. Don't talk to me about giving back, fuck these streets! It's always about financial gain."

"Are we doing this shit or not?" I guess Fresh was getting tired of the back and forth.

"Let's vote." Wise wanted this bad.

So now everybody is looking at me. I could easily kill this shit with one word, but I'm not going to do that. I need everybody on the same side; for now anyway.

"Ok, let's vote. Who wants to play superhero?"

One by one they raised their hands. Ant hesitated but still had his hand straight up in the air. I shook my head looking at all of them but when I got to Wise he was smiling at me. He was loving this shit and I had no choice but to go along with it.

"Dummies. I hope y'all capes are made of Teflon."

"Fuck you Chase!" Wise stood up.

"No, fuck you!" I jumped up to.

Now everybody is up from the table. Fresh and Spazz kept me and Wise from getting to each other.

"Come on man! You two need to cut this shit out; For real." Ant was mad as hell.

"Meetings over!" I didn't want to look at none of them anymore.

"Chase?" Ant looked at me like he was confused.

"Meetings over!" I screamed in his face.

Fresh and Spazz both wait until Wise nods his head at them to leave and all three of them go out of the door together. Chino followed behind them still pissed off that he won't be going with me and Ant to take care of Cuco. Ant doesn't leave; he sits back down and leans back in the chair. I knew he wasn't going to go anywhere until he got whatever it was off his chest so I sat back down.

"What's going on with you and your pops man?" Ant spoke first.

"I'm getting tired of hearing that."

"What, that he's your pops? He's the closet thing you've had to one."

"I'm getting tired of hearing that to."

"I've known you a long time man. You can't tell me you don't see Wise as your pops."

"I shot at him this morning."

"You shot at him? What the fuck for?"

"It doesn't matter; he needed to know he's not exempt.

Ant looked at me like I was crazy. He was getting ready to speak when we heard people running up the stairs. The door opened and Wise walked in; the crew was behind him plus one.

"We got a problem." Wise stepped to the side so I could see the girl that Spazz and Fresh was holding on to.

"Who is this? I almost didn't want to ask.

"Like I said, we have a problem." Wise said again.

"She was sitting in car up the street watching the building. She wasn't hard to spot." Fresh spoke up.

"This is not good Chase; we need to kill this bitch!" Spazz was excited.

I got up from my chair, walked over and looked at this chick. She had a pale white complexion with short black hair. She wasn't from around here.

"Who are you?

"My name is Cali." She spoke with a slight accent.

"Hi Cali, what can I do for you?"

"Your intentions with Cuco are not in your best interest."

"So you're the one tailing Cuco."

"Yes. I'm from Miami."

"You couldn't tell she was the one following him?" Wise looked at Chino.

"It was dark, I couldn't see." Chino put his head down.

"So what is in my best interest Cali?" I was interested in what she had to say.

"To let Cuco deliver his product back to Miami."

"See that's a problem. It's not his product."

"Don't interfere."

"That sounds like a threat Cali."

"Take it how you want."

"See, we need to kill this bitch now!" Spazz was ready.

"Chill." Fresh tried to calm Spazz down.

"You have a lot of heart Cali but I think it's in your best interest to leave before you can't." I wanted to know what her connection was to Cuco but I knew I would have to wait.

"Chase, you won't get another warning. The man I represent won't allow you to interfere."

"That's good because I don't like warnings and as for the man you represent. Tell him a man that hides behind a woman is a coward."

"Ok." She smiled at me.

"This is trouble, we need to handle this." Ant whispered in my ear.

"What you want us to do Chase?" Fresh was getting impatient.

"Let her go."

"Let her go? That's crazy! We can't let her walk out of here. I got this, let me handle this." Spazz was turning into a beast.

"Relax Spazz." Wise slapped Spazz in the chest.

"He's right. I should kill you." I said looking at Cali.

"Killing me will only ensure the deaths of all of you."

"You're a long way from home Cali, be careful. Talking like that will ensure that you never make it back to Miami. It would be safer for you to try and be my friend."

"I'm not looking to be your friend Chase. I'm here for one reason only and that's to make sure Cuco gets back to Miami, safely."

"Let her go." I said again looking at Fresh and Spazz.

Fresh loosened his grip on Cali's arm but Spazz didn't budge.

"Did you hear what I said?" I said looking at Spazz.

Spazz reluctantly let her go but she didn't move. She stood there looking at each one of us until Spazz lost it and pushed her in the direction of the door.

"Get the fuck out of here before something bad happens to you!" Spazz was yelling now.

Wise had to step in the middle and pull Spazz back.

"You're free to go Cali. I'm sure we'll see each other again and I look forward to it." I said smiling at her.

"Follow her." Wise looked over at Fresh.

Fresh nods and walks out with Spazz right behind him but Wise stopped him by grabbing his arm.

"Just follow her, don't touch her." Wise looked at Spazz seriously.

"Yea, yea, yea." Spazz pulled away from Wise and ran behind Fresh.

Wise took a deep breath then turned my direction and gave me one of his concerned looks.

"What?" I asked.

"What you plan on doing?

"Nothing changes."

"You need to find out who these people are." Wise looked worried.

"I have a feeling I'm going to find out soon enough."

"You should find out first before you play a game you might not win."

"I got this POPS!" I tapped him on the chest and walked away.

Wise walked out and Chino followed behind him.

"This isn't good Chase." Ant started pacing.

"None of this shit is good but when has it ever been."

"What about you and Wise?"

"Fuck him."

"Maybe the problem isn't him Chase, maybe it's you. You ever think that?"

"Nope."

"You can say what you want but you wouldn't kill him. He's family and that makes him exempt."

I just looked at Ant without saying a word. He laughed then shook his head.

"What about me Chase? Am I exempt?"

"No ones exempt."

I got up from the table and walked out the back door. I could hear his footsteps following behind me. There was a fire burning in a garbage can in the back of the building. I used the flames to light my black n mild. Ant walked around me and lit a cigarette, staring at me like he had something else on his mind. My phone rang.

"Who's this?" I asked answering the phone.

"We need to talk."

"Who's this?" I said again.

"The man you're trying to kill."

I laughed.

"Listen, let me get back to Miami and I promise I won't come back." Cuco was a bold man.

"You should have never come out here to begin with." I hung up.

"Who was that?" Ant was curious.

"Cuco."

"Cuco? How the fuck did he get your number?"

"Cali did her homework."

"You should have killed her when you had the chance Chase."

"Catch up with Fresh and Spazz and find out where she went."

"Ok, where you going?"

"Home for a little bit. I'll catch up with you later."

Ant left and my phone rang again.

"Yea." I answered.

"Chase?"

"Yea Papo, What's up?"

"Change of plans. Cuco is not to be touched."

"Why? What happened?"

"I've changed my mind. That's all you need to know."

He hung up. I stood there looking at my phone, this didn't feel right. What made him change his mind? I need to figure this out. I called Ant and told him to get in touch with everybody and tell them the plans were put on hold then I went home.

CHASE
CHAPTER FOUR

"What's good Chase?" Chino walked up just as I was lighting my black n mild.

"What's up Chino?"

"How was the meeting with my pops?

"It went good. Looks like we're going to be working together."

"Cool. There is something I want to talk to you about though."

"What's that?"

"Why do you keep shutting me out of a lot of shit?"

"Because I don't think you can handle it. You're not built for war Chino."

"How do you know when you ain't giving me a chance?"

I stared at Chino for a minute.

"Ok, me and Wise have to plan the move on the dude that raped that girl. I'll make sure you'll get a chance to put some work in."

"Cool. Now my other question."

"What's up?"

"What you doing tonight? I got somebody I want you to meet."

"I don't like the sound of that Chino."

"It's a girl. A friend of mine just moved back to Jersey from Virginia. You're going to like her; she's really pretty and down to earth."

"You hit it?"

"No man, she's my friend."

"What does that mean?"

"It's not like that Chase. We grew up together, she's like my sister."

"If you say so. No thanks though. I can get my own pussy."

"I'm not trying to get you pussy. She's a good girl. Just thought you might want to meet her. A few of us going out for drinks later on. You can slide through and see for yourself."

"Where y'all going to be?"

"Club Atmosphere."

"We'll see what happens."

"Ok, so I'll catch you later. Don't forget about me Chase, I really want to show you guys that I can handle anything you throw at me."

"I got you."

My phone started ringing so I nodded at Chino who walked away.

"Yea" I answered.

"Chase?"

"Yea Ant."

"You need me tonight?"

"Absolutely."

"You picking me up?"

"Yea, I'll be there at eight?"

"Ight."

I hung up with Ant and went back in the house. I needed to talk to Wise about this plan to take care of these dudes.

"Wise!"

"What?"

"Come out here!" I yelled standing outside his bedroom door.

I went back into the living room and fell back on the couch. About ten minutes later, Wise walked in.

"What you need Chase?"

"I needed for you not to have me sitting out here so damn long."

"I had to get dressed or did you want me to come out here with my dick swinging? "

"Never interested in seeing your dick."

"I didn't think so. So what's up?"

"Since you got the vote on taking care of this non profit situation we need to go over how we going to handle it."

"True. The dude hangs out at the car wash on 18th ave."

"He got people backing him up?"

"Yea but they not deep, it's about three or four of them but there are other cats that hang out there getting their money to."

"Ok, so how you want to handle this Wise. You want walk up to them and politely challenge them to a boxing match?"

"You're a funny man. No, my plan was to run up on all of them and take out whoever is out there."

"Oh shit so now you're about the violence?"

"I'm just not with unnecessary violence."

"Whatever. Listen Chino wants more work. He came to me earlier about wanting to prove to us he can handle himself.

"So he's ready to really put some work in? That what's up. Shit, it's about time. Let's give him a chance to be the front runner on this one."

"I don't give a shit. So be it."

"Ok. So all the stores close around 9pm on 18th ave. The car wash stays open till about 11pm. So we make it our business to be out there by twelve. The car wash is in between Alexander and West End. We going to flood them from both sides."

"When you want to do this Wise?"

"I want to do it tonight."

"Too soon."

"Why?"

"Because you're going to have to go over the details with the team Wise, especially if you going to have Chino be the front runner. That fool might shoot himself if he's not careful besides me and Ant going to do a little surveillance tonight."

"On who?'

"Papo, I don't like how he just changed his mind about Cuco, something is up with that. I want to see who I'm doing business with."

"You mean who *we're* doing business with."

"Whatever."

"So tomorrow it is."

"Yea, just let the guys know we need to meet up tomorrow."

"I'm on it and by the way. Mu and Kane are on board."

"Oh really? They know the terms?"

"Chase, what did I tell you? I got them covered. No worries."

"Ok I'm out. I'll see you later."

I had some time to kill so I took a ride and stopped at the liquor store to grab a bottle. This whole Mu and Kane shit wasn't sitting right with me. It felt like Wise was bringing them in as a power move. Yea they make our team stronger but what was Wise really trying to do? Before I knew it, I was in Queens. I come out here to think and to get away from everybody and everything. I parked my car and walked into the cemetery. I walked over and stood in front of my mother's and father's plots which was side by side. I sat down in between them, rested my head on my father's tombstone and started drinking. This was the only place I found peace. The only place I wasn't paranoid. There was a funeral going on and I could see people standing over the casket of whoever died. I wonder how many people will be at my funeral. There was a woman singing, I don't know the name of the song but she was singing about walking around heaven, I doubt they will be singing that at my funeral. I got so comfortable that I fell asleep, when I woke up, that funeral was over. It was time for me to head back. Instead of leaving flowers, I left the empty bottle. I jumped in my car and headed back to Jersey. Ant was already outside when I pulled up. He jumped in and I drove to Papo's house.

"Did you catch up with Spazz and Fresh last night?"

"Yea I did Chase."

"Ok, and?"

"They followed Cali to some motel on 1&9 which I don't understand. Why would she choose to stay in a dump?"

"She wants to stay low key, out of sight. We definitely need to keep an eye on her."

"Whatever."

"What's your problem Ant?"

"I don't have a problem."

"Stop acting like a bitch and say what's on your mind."

"What's on my mind is that shit you said to me last night."

"You still on that?"

"Chase, your mindset is crazy. You talk about killing people who are your family. I'm your best friend but you tell me that no one is exempt."

We were getting close to Papo's house so I parked close enough to see his front door and driveway. I turned the car off including the lights and sat back in my seat then looked at Ant.

"Family? Ant. My aunt killed my mother and years later, I killed her. That was blood; born from the same bloodline and it didn't mean shit in the end. Your like a brother to me but if put in a position where I had to take your life, I will."

"That means you have no soul Chase."

"Ant you grew up the same way I did. You saw the same shit. How could you not understand where I'm coming from?"

"I believe in family Chase and you should to, especially when it comes to Wise."

"I don't want to hear that father bullshit anymore. Wise is your family, not mine."

"He treated us the same growing up and you know that. He's my mom's cousin but he still treated me like I was his son, just like he did you."

"You ever ask him what happened to your father?"

"Why would I ask him about my father?

"I don't know."

"Don't fuck around with me Chase. My moms told me that my pops left us and never looked back."

"Norey lied to you."

"What the fuck are you talking about Chase?"

"Wait, look. Who's that?"

I saw a car pulling into Papo's driveway.

"Whoever it is, they're driving to the back of the house."

"Shit, I'm trying to see if I can see the plate number."

"Is it Jersey plates?"

"Yea, it's BWN45P. Write it down Ant."

"Got it."

"Good. Take it to your moms. Ask her to check the dmv records for us."

"Ok. Now tell me what you know about my father."

"Before we left Atlanta. I overheard Wise talking to your pops."

"What? How?"

"I was hanging with Wise one night, he said he had to make a stop. He pulled up in front of a bar and told me to stay in the car. You know me, I got tired of waiting and went inside. The place was damn near empty so I went to the back. I could hear Wise and somebody else talking. Wise was this dude that his relationship with Norey was over and that he had one chance to leave Atlanta. He said that if he ever caught him around his cousin again that he would kill him and anybody that cared about him."

Ant didn't say anything.

"You ok Ant?"

"No, I'm not ok. Why didn't you tell me this shit before?"

"It wasn't my story to tell. I'm only telling you now because I'm tired of hearing you talk about Wise like he's your hero."

"Even if what your saying is true; he's still family Chase."

"Fuck family."

"What about Trisha?"

"Trisha is the only exception."

"So you're not completely heartless."

"I'm what I was made to be."

"What the does that mean?"

"It means watch the fucking house and stop running your mouth."

A few minutes later the car pulled out and left. The windows were tinted, we couldn't see anything. Hopefully Norey can tell us more information from the plate number. It was quiet in the car for a few minutes. I know Ant was feeling confused and pissed from the information I gave him about his pops but he needed to know the truth. Wise was the reason his father wasn't around and I hope Ant grows some balls and confronts him on that. We were still sitting there when Chino came home. I shook my head watching Chino's drunken ass trying to get in his house. His sister snatched the door open and Chino stumbled inside. A few minutes later we saw her leave with her friends. I started to pull off when a cab pulled up. Me and Ant both sat up straight to see who it was. We laughed when it was Cali that got out of the cab.

"So what now Chase?"

"We don't do anything yet. I'm going to let this one play out, see what happens but now it makes sense why he changed his mind about Cuco."

"What do you think he's planning?"

"I don't know but I'm definitely going to find out. You feel like going to get a drink?"

"Why not? Fuck it."

"Chino's at Atmosphere with some chicks."

"Ok, let's go."

CHASE
CHAPTER FIVE

We pulled up to the club and it was crazy. All you saw was chicks with damn near nothing on and dudes breaking their necks to get close to them. Parking was crazy but I finally found a spot not too far from the door. We jumped out and headed in.

"Damn it's a lot of people out here." Ant was saying out loud what I was thinking in my head.

"Yea and they all dressed like they're going to some major event instead of a club in the middle of the hood.

"Maybe we should have gotten dressed up to."

"T shirts and jeans are dressy. Just don't look anybody in the eye and if anybody approaches you just show them your gun."

"You're a clown."

I immediately saw Chino at the bar.

"There's Chino. Come on."

Ant was was walking behind me. He was so busy staring at all the ass that was around that he kept bumping into me.

"My bad Chase."

We both laughed.

"What's good Chino?" I shook his hand.

"Chino!" Ant hugged him.

I leaned over the bar and told the bartender to bring us some shots of Remy.

"What's up fellas? The girls just went to the bathroom. Sophie got excited when I described you Chase.

"Oh yea? How did you describe me?"

"I just told her that you were 6'1, light brown complexion and so many tats that your skin is probably made of ink."

"Funny."

"And Ant don't worry it's three of them so you won't be lonely. Here they come now. Sophie is the one in the front."

Sophie had a mocha complexion, looked about 5'9 with those heels on. She was already smiling by the time she got to me.

"Sophie, Nicole and Alexandria these are my boys Chase and Ant."

"Hi Chase, nice to meet you." Sophie got real close to me.

"What's up Sophie? Nice to meet you to." She was cute, tonight might not be a waste of time after all.

Ant paired up with Alexandria since Chino claimed Nicole. I kept the shots coming; I wanted to see how Sophie handled her liquor. She laughed a lot and stumbled a couple of times but she didn't act stupid.

"What do you do Sophie?" I asked really not giving two shits but wanted to keep a conversation going.

"I'm a paralegal. What do you do?"

"I work for myself." I said smiling.

"I'm scared to even ask what that means."

I laughed.

"So where you from Sophie?"

"Montclair, I like how you changed the subject."

"You liked that? I thought you would."

"Hey Chase, did you talk to Wise for me?" Chino asked putting his hand on my shoulder.

"Yea Chino, we'll talk about that later."

"Ok no problem. Where are the drinks?"

"Damn Chino, chill out. You looking like you might not need anymore." Ant started laughing.

"You chill out Ant, I'm good."

Chino had to be drunk to talk to me about business in front of these chicks. That's definitely something we don't do. He walked off in the direction of the bathroom, stumbling and bumping into people on the way.

"Ant, Chino's drunk. Keep your eyes open."

"I'm already on it."

It wasn't long before we heard Chino's slurred voice arguing with somebody that he probably bumped into.

"Fuck you motherfucker! You don't want any problems with me! Me and my boys will shut this place down!"

Chino was out of control and talking real reckless to a man that was 10 times his weight and about 5 feet taller than him. Ant was on his way to rescue him but I stopped him.

"Let him handle his own shit. Let's see what he's made of."

"Chase do you see how big that dude is?"

"So what, he has to learn to handle his own business."

Chino was feeling strong; he pushed the dude who didn't budge an inch. This man hit Chino so hard that Chino hit the floor and slid all the way back to where we was standing. I wanted to laugh looking down at him but I didn't. Me and Ant helped him off the floor and carried his ass outside with the girls running behind us.

"Fuck that Chase. Let's go back in and get those motherfuckers!" Chino couldn't even hold his head up while he was talking.

"You can't even walk straight, shut up. Which one of you girls drove?" I was trying not to get mad.

"I did." Alexandria answered.

"Take him home."

"Ok, come on Chino." Alexandria and Nicole grabbed Chino, dragging him to the car. Sophie slowly walked behind them.

"Not you Sophie. Take my keys and go sit in my car. I'll be there in a couple of minutes. It's the black charger across the street."

"Ok." She smiled and took the keys.

Me and Ant both knew that it wasn't over so we stood outside waiting and just like we expected the dude and his friends came running out.

"Where's your friend?" The big dude asked.

"He left. Why don't you go back inside."

"We'll go back inside when you pay for my drink that your friend made me spill."

"Well that's not going to happen."

"Then you're going to have to take this ass whooping for your friend!"

"Listen man. We're not looking for any trouble. Just go back inside and enjoy the rest of your night." Ant was trying to be nice.

I stepped back a little to give me space between me and the giant because I saw what was coming next. Ant unfortunately didn't move in enough time and got hit with the punch the big guy threw. The punch was sloppy though, Ant only stumbled back a little bit. I reacted quickly and swung hard enough to knock this dude to the ground which wasn't hard because he was drunk. Ant pulled his gun out and pointed it at the guy's friends who were up until that moment ready to revenge their friends knock out but the gun made them change their minds.

"Let's go Ant." I said tapping the extended arm with the gun in it.

"Goodnight Fellas." Ant waved bye to the guys.

"Y'all ok?" Sophie asked when we got in the car.

"Yea we're good."

"Alexandria called me and told me they dropped Chino off at home."

"Cool."

I dropped Ant off and took Sophie back to my house. When we walked in Trisha and Norey was sitting on the couch drinking and laughing.

“What y'all laughing at?”

“Hey Chase, I was telling Trisha old stories about your mom.”

“Oh okay. Sophie, these are my Aunts Trisha and Norey.”

Trisha and Norey didn’t say anything at first. I was waiting for Trisha to say some slick shit but she was quiet.

“Sophie where are you from?” Norey started asking questions.

“Montclair.”

“Okay, what do you do?”

“I’m a paralegal.”

“Really? How did you meet Chase, in court?” Norey started laughing which caused Trisha to start laughing.

I just shook my head at their drunken asses.

“Chino introduced me to him.”

“So you’re friends with Chino. Is he a good friend?” Trisha finally spoke up.

“Yea, he is.”

“I would question his friendship if I were you. Good luck sweetie.” Trisha looked at me and started laughing again.

I pulled Sophie away from them and we went into my room. I could still hear Trisha and Norey laughing until I closed the door. I took Sophie's jacket out of her hands and tossed it on the chair I had in the corner of the room.

"Your aunts are funny."

"Yea, Norey really isn't my aunt. She's Ant's moms but she been around me all my life."

"That's sweet. Do you introduce every girl you meet to your aunts?"

"Yea I do."

"What? Are you serious?"

"Yea I am. Is there something wrong with that?"

"No, I guess. I just wasn't expecting you to say that."

"We're you expecting me to say, you're the first girl that I've brought around my family?"

"No I wasn't expecting that but, you know what? Never mind."

"Are you upset now?"

"No but maybe I should go home."

She walked over and grabbed her jacket and started walking towards the door. I got to her before she could open it. She turned around with an attitude and one eyebrow raised.

"What's the problem?" I couldn't help but smile at her. This was fun for me.

"No problem. I just want to go home."

"Why? Because your used to people lying to you?

"I'm not used to anybody lying to me. I'm just not use to someone being so brutally honest."

"Take what I said to you as a show of respect. I respect you enough to tell you the truth."

"Chase, how many girls are you dealing with?"

"How is knowing that information going to help us get to know each other better?"

"I just want to know where I'm going to stand with you."

"Listen, none of that matters at this point and time. You're here because you wanted to get to know me, right?"

"Yes."

"So get to know me."

I took her by the hand and walked her over to the bed. I sat down and made her stand in front of me. I took her jacket and her bag out of her hand, tossing them across the room. I liked the way she was looking at me, you could tell she was scared. I started unbuttoning the white button up shirt she had on, she started breathing heavy. Sophie's shyness lasted for about a minute. With her shirt now off she bent down in front of me. Her hands were under my shirt caressing my chest while she kissed me like she was ready. I took her bra off with no effort and she stood up and took her jeans. Her body was nice, I liked the way she looked naked. She took my shirt off and ran her hands over my tattoos. I slid my hand in between her legs and pushed two of my fingers inside of her, she moaned. The faster my hand moved the faster her breathing got. I played with her until she couldn't take it anymore and exploded all over my hand. I laid down on the bed and pulled her body on top of mines. She put me inside of her and moved like a professional. I laid back and enjoyed the view. Her eyes rolled in the back of her head and her movements got faster. I thought she was about to start jumping up and down on me. She was so wet, I had no choice but to give in. Everything I had built up, I let loose inside of her.

CHASE
CHAPTER SIX

"We only got a few hours before this shit goes down. First thing I want to do is welcome Kane and Mu to the team. We'll discuss their roles at the next meeting. Right now Wise is going to lay out what we're doing tonight. Wise you got the floor."

"Ok fellas, they call this dude Zee. He's a dirty looking motherfucker. You'll recognize him when you see him. He's got long dirty looking dreads and a long dirty looking beard. Spazz you and Fresh are going to be on West End. Ant I want you to park at the end of that block. Spazz, all you and Fresh have to do is walk down to 18th ave but pace yourselves, walk slowly. That block is quiet so you shouldn't have any problems; nobody is usually out there late night. Me and Chase are going to be on Alexander. Chino, you're point man on this so be on point! There's a liquor store across the street from the car wash. I want you to go in and buy a double shot of E&J and say to the dude behind the counter, I need that."

"Say, I need what Wise?"

"Chino, just say I need that. He'll know what you're talking about."

"Oh ok."

"He's going to nod to one of Zee's boys that will already be in the store. The dude he nods to will walk up to you and ask you what you need. Tell him one."

"One what?"

"One bag."

"A bag of what?"

I wanted to laugh because I knew that Chino was going to fuck this up.

"Chino, you getting a bag of dope." Wise was getting aggravated

"Oh shit. They going to believe I'm buying a bag of dope?"

"I would. You could easily pass for a dirty white boy so why not a dirty white boy who's a dope head." I said shaking my head at Chino.

"Ha-ha, ok." Chino was laughing but he looked scared to me.

"Dude is going to walk out of the store. Stay there and don't move. Another dude is going to come back in with the dope. Give him the money, take the dope and leave. Walk straight to Alexander and walk up."

"Ok, that's it?"

"Yea. At that point dude number one would have already told Zee that he has a new customer since they've never seen you around before. Zee is paranoid. He doesn't trust anybody so he's going to follow you when you come out of the store. He lives on Alexander so when he sees you going up his block, he's going to want to know where your going. This shit has to be timed right. As soon as he starts walking up Alexander Street, Spazz and Fresh you guys got to be on it. I want you to spray everything moving. Chino walk straight pass me and Chase to where Ant is. Kane and Mu will make sure nobody from around the neighborhood gets involved. Me and Chase will take care of everything else."

"How is Mu and Kane going to do that?" Chino asked looking confused.

"Kane? You want to answer Chino's question?" Wise looked like he was tired of talking to Chino.

"Chino, it won't be any peace if they get involved and they know that. They don't want a war with us." Kane made his point quick.

I have to admit that Wise's plan sounded good and everybody knew exactly what they were supposed to do and when they were supposed to do it. The whole time

Wise was talking my phone was blowing up. The first time it went off, I looked at it and it was Sophie. I ignored it but it's been going off ever since. That shit was pissing me off but I had to get my mind back on the meeting.

"Ok, the next matter on the table is Cali. Me and Ant saw her going in Papo's house last night which has to be the reason Papo is holding off on taking care of Cuco. I want to find out what they're up to. We got some time so Spazz and Fresh I want you to go to that motel you followed her to and see if you can shake somebody into telling you how long she been there and if she's had any visitors."

"We're on it."

Spazz and Fresh jumped up and was out the door. Mu and Kane was next to leave and Wise sent Chino home to change his clothes. I stepped out of the room and pulled my phone out to call Sophie.

"Hello."

"What's up Sophie? This is Chase."

"Hey you. I know who this is."

"I saw that you called me a few thousand times. You ok?"

"Your funny, I just wanted to know if I was going to see you tonight."

"Listen baby girl, if you call me and I don't answer then wait for me to call you back. On most days, I'm busy so that phone constantly buzzing in my pocket pisses me off if I'm trying to take care of something.

"Oh I'm sorry, I just miss you and wanted to hear your voice."

I paused and moved the phone from my ear. I looked at it for a second. I wanted to hang up on her but I didn't. I kept cool

"I've got a few things to take care of then I'll call you back."

"Oh ok, I was thinking maybe you could come over here and I'll cook you dinner."

"You don't have to cook for me Sophie but I might slide through. I'll hit you back in a few, ok?"

"Ok."

I hung up and went back in the room with Wise and Ant.

"Ight, we need to get into position soon so Ant hit me when you got Spazz and Fresh. Wise I'll meet you back at the house in a couple of hours."

I shook hands with Ant and nodded my head at Wise. I called Sophie back and told her I would be there in a few minutes. My mind was on Cali though. It didn't feel right. What did she offer Papo to make him change his mind about Cuco?

"Hey handsome." Sophie said opening the door with a big smile on her face.

"What's up Sophie?"

I walked in her living room and looked around her apartment before sitting down on the couch."

"You want a tour?"

"Yea, where's the bedroom?"

"You play around too much." She was laughing.

"I was serious."

"Hush, let me show you around."

"Sophie, come here."

She came closer and I made her sit on my lap. She put her hand on my face and I had my hand up her shirt unhooking her bra.

"Damn Chase, I don't even get a kiss first or maybe a hug? You just want to get straight to it."

"I don't have a lot of time Sophie."

"So why didn't you come after you finished doing what you had to do?"

"I'm here now. You want me to leave and come back later?"

"No."

"Then take this off."

I pulled at her shirt and she took it off. I pulled at her jeans she had on and she stood up and took those off to.

"You happy now?" She asked.

"Nope."

I sat back on the couch, slid down to get comfortable and unzipped my jeans. She smiled at me like she was waiting for me to say something. I looked down and then looked at her. It took her a couple of seconds to get the hint but when she did, she got on her knees. I pushed her head back down every time she came up for air. I grabbed her hair with both of my hands pushing her head down harder until I felt like I was close to her tonsils. She was gagging and choking and it was making me want to bust.

"Chase, don't cum in my mouth." She was trying to talk with her mouth full of dick.

"Shhhhhh." I pushed her head back down.

My movements got faster and she was trying to keep up. I could feel the spit sliding out of her mouth onto my tip. I grabbed her head again but this time held it in one place. She tried to pull her head up but that wasn't an option. I exploded in her mouth and she had no choice but to swallow what was in her mouth. She jumped up with her mouth flooded. She ran into the bathroom and a couple minutes later came back out, mad.

"What's wrong with you Chase? I told you not to cum in my mouth!"

"My bad."

I got up and went into the bathroom to clean up, I waited till I got in the bathroom to laugh. Women kill me with that shit. If you sucking my dick then I'm going to cum in you mouth, simple as that. When I came out the bathroom she was sitting there looking at me strange.

"Chase?"

"What?"

"What are we doing?"

"What do you mean?"

"I mean, I don't want to be just some jump off to you."

"Sophie, I just met you."

"I know that. I'm just saying, I want more."

"I don't have time for more right now and right about now, I got to go."

"When are you coming back?"

"When I can."

"When is that?"

"I'll call you Sophie."

I kissed her on the cheek and got the fuck out of there. I drove to the house and picked up Wise."

"What's up Chase? Have you heard from Ant yet?"

"Not yet."

"Let's go get Chino."

"Alright."

By the time we got to Chino; I got Ant's call. Spazz and Fresh was in the car with him. Wise got a call from Mu letting him know that everything was good and that they would be in the vicinity if we needed them. Chino looked the part. His jeans were dirty and the white T-shirt he had on was dingy. His hair was all over his head and you could even see some dirt on his face. He was pale so the dirt was definitely noticeable. Wise turned around to face Chino in the back seat.

"You good Chino?"

"Yea I'm good Wise. I'm not going to fuck this up. I promise."

"That's good cause if they think they being set up they will put a bullet in your head."

"I understand."

"Good." Wise turned back around in his seat.

So here we go. I parked my car behind Ant's on West End and left the keys in it. Once this is over with, we're going to need to get out of here fast. Chino got out first and me and Wise waited about five minutes then got out to. We stopped and laid low about halfway down the block; we could see Chino real good from where we was at. I was surprised that Chino didn't look nervous; hopefully he makes it back up this block.

"Chase, stay here I'm going to walk down and make sure this kid doesn't get killed."

"No Wise, he wants to prove that he's built for this, so let him prove it."

"Yea and what if they blow his head off?"

"Then we'll know that he wasn't cut out for it."

"That's fucked up. If Chino dies then so does your partnership with Papo."

"This is business not personal, Papo knows that."

"I'm not willing to take that chance Chase, let's move closer."

We went through the backyards until we got to a closer spot and by that time shit was already going down. One dude came out of the store, nodded to another dude who walked around the corner, behind the store. At the same time, the first dude walks over to Zee and now they're talking. From around the corner the second dude comes back and goes into the store. A couple of minutes later, Chino comes out. So far so good.

"Hey!" Zee called out to Chino.

"Here we go Chase. Zee is calling Chino."

"Wait Wise, wait and see what happens."

Chino walked over to Zee; you could see the fear all over his face. We couldn't hear what they were saying but obviously Zee didn't like Chino's response because a second later Zee grabbed Chino by the shirt and had him almost dangling by his feet. It was over for the kid, Chino was about to die; at least that's what I thought but Chino wasn't going out just yet. Chino swung wildly at Zee, he didn't connect with any of his punches but he managed to pull away from Zee and free himself. Zee was standing there still holding onto Chino's shirt as Chino hauled ass in our direction, shirtless. Zee and his boys of course started shooting at him and that was our queue. Me and Wise ran out from behind the house, guns already drawn and throwing bullets in the directions of anyone we saw standing to make sure Chino could get away. He's lucky he didn't hesitate, look back or stop because that would have been the end of him. Fresh and Spazz was already on the ave making sure Zee's boys didn't make it off the block. Zee jumped into a Ford Taurus and took off. We ran behind the car shooting; Wise must have hit him because the car ran into the McDonalds parking lot hitting a pole. We got to the car just in enough time to see Zee lift his head off of the steering wheel. Wise shot him twice, Zee laid his head back down. Chino pulled up on the side of us in my car and we jumped in. I looked over at him and bust out laughing, he was sweating and looked like he had been crying.

"You ight Chino?" Wise was talking from the back seat.

"Yea I'm good. Cold but good."

"Chino pull my car over man. You're driving reckless as hell." I wasn't about to let him crash my car.

"I'm sorry Chase, I guess I'm a little nervous."

Once we switched seats, I called Ant to make sure everybody was good which they were. I dropped Chino off then me and Wise went home.

CHASE
CHAPTER SEVEN

"Last night was crazy man!" Spazz opened our meeting.

"Listen I don't think I'm going to ever get that image of Chino running up the block with no shirt on out of my head." Wise said looking at Chino laughing.

"I'm not going to lie man, I was scared shitless." Chino had to laugh at himself.

"Ok, so now that our community service is done let's get back to business. Spazz did y'all find out anything at that motel that Cali is at? I still had that shit with Papo on my mind.

"Not much Chase. The guy that runs it said she goes out for a little bit but comes right back. She's quiet and stays to herself, no visitors."

"Still keep an eye on her. I want to know everything that she does."

"You got it Chase."

"Now we can talk about our new members to the team and what the goal is. Wise you want to start us off?" I turned the meeting over to Wise.

"Ok, let me give you guys a little background info. Mu and Kane are family. Chase and Ant was kids when they met these two but me? These are my brothers, been my boys my whole life. All three of us are originally from Jersey where we started our crew. What we did last night for Denise Johnson was what we did for a living among other things but there was more of us back then. That's how we met Chase but that was a long time ago. Their main business now is guns and cars. Matter of fact Kane, I'm going to let you continue from here."

Kane cleared his throat like he was about to make a speech.

"Ok, so like Wise said the three of us originate from Jersey. This is home for us and where all our guns come from even when we was in Atlanta but before we left and went to Atlanta we had a small crew of car thieves that at first stole cars just for fun but we taught them how to turn that into money. My boy Jay, rest in peace, recruited smart kids that weren't about being broke. When we left to go to Atlanta Jay knew that we were going to still need our team secure in Jersey so he ran it from Atlanta. When he died I took it over and later on Mu came on board. We got a chop shop in North Newark. The Spanish homies are good at what they do."

"So y'all sell stolen car parts?" Fresh asked.

"Something like that. We don't steal high end cars. We get mostly American cars. Cars that don't have expensive parts. We fix what needs to be fixed; we repaint, put a new VIN number on it and put it back on the street for sale." Kane said sitting back in his chair.

"Damn, ight. Where y'all getting the cars from?"Spazz's question was next.

"Montclair, Maplewood, South Orange. Places like that?

"What about the cops? I heard they are strict up in those areas." Chino asked.

"Mu, you can take that question." Kane laughed a little looking at Mu.

"Ha-ha, yea the cops are strict up there but they also crooked as fuck. When we got out to Atlanta, I wanted to change my life so I joined the police dept. I found out that cops were the most crooked motherfuckers alive. That's not what I was about but it taught me a lot about how they think. Once we got back to Jersey it was easy getting the local cops to look the other way. They all just wanted to get paid. Now the problem we have is the Train."

"What the fuck is the train?" I was curious.

"Chase, the Train is a group of officers specifically put on the street to stop stolen cars by any means necessary. They ride around in trucks with crash bars for the main purpose of hitting you and making you crash or worse, killing you."

"A license to kill." I shook my head.

"Exactly Chase. They will push you into a brick wall if they can. If you get caught up with them and can't get away then it's a wrap. That's our issue right now. We lost four drivers in the last couple of weeks."

"So what you need from us?" I was hoping they didn't want us to drive for them. We have enough cops on our asses already.

"We need more bodies on the street. We need to know when the Train is coming, give our drivers enough time to get the hell out of there."

"I thought ya'll had the streets locked."

"Chase, we do when it comes to the hustlers but the cops are a different story plus we need people we can trust to have our backs."

"Ok, that's easy enough. Welcome to the team men. Is there anything else for the table?" I was ready to wrap this up.

"How about we break out that Remy bottle Chase been hiding in here for the past week?" Spazz ran into the kitchen and grabbed the bottle from under the counter.

"How do you know where that bottle was? I forgot that shit was even in here.

"I can smell liquor a mile away Chase." Wise was laughing.

"Ok, open it up." I gave in.

Once we started drinking we didn't stop until the bottle was empty. We drank and talked shit for the rest of the night. Chino of course was the drunkest.

"Chino, why can't you hold your liquor?" Ant asked him laughing.

"I'm not drunk, I'm relaxed. Give me some more."

"There is no more! You drank it all." I was laughing to.

"Ok let's go get more Chase. I love the sound of a bottle opening. It's the best sound in the world."

"Yea, Chino is definitely fucked up. First off the best sound in the world is salsa music on a hot day." Spazz stood up and was dancing with himself.

"Why a hot day Spazz?" Fresh asked interested.

"Cause when the ladies are dancing, they sweat. Sometimes you can see the sweat dripping down their legs and if you stand close enough you might even be lucky enough to get hit with some of that sweat."

The whole room paused for a minute to just look at Spazz then we all lost it and started laughing.

"I always knew Spazz was nasty as hell. Fresh! what's your favorite sound?" Wise was having fun.

"The sound of a gun being cocked back."

"Ha-ha. Ok, I like that. Ant what's yours? Wise was going around the room.

"The sound of my mom in the kitchen cooking."

"That's because your ass is greedy. Wise, what about you? Spazz turned to Wise.

"The sound my woman makes when I'm inside her."

"Come on man, I don't want to hear that shit." I was disgusted.

"She might be your aunt but she's my woman."

"I still don't want to hear that. Mu, your up." I needed to change that conversation quick.

"Man my favorite sound is my alarm. Waking up everyday is a blessing."

"That's corny as hell but that's you Mu. What about you Kane?" I looked over at Kane.

Mu stuck his middle finger up at me.

"My favorite sound is the lighter when I'm about to burn some trees and speaking of trees, it's time for me to go. Take care fellas. "Kane got up and left.

Everyone laughed and shook Kane's hand as he was leaving.

"Chino! What's your favorite sound? I looked over at Chino.

"Chino is knocked the fuck out Chase." Chino's head was back and Fresh was poking him in the ribs but he wasn't budging.

"I'm not taking that fool home so I hope one of y'all got him." I wasn't playing cab tonight.

"I'll take him home. Fresh said as him and Spazz stood over Chino just staring at him.

"Ok good, I'm about to be out to." I stood up.

"Hold up Chase! It's your turn, you haven't told us what your favorite sound is." Spazz was loving this.

"The sound of a person taking their last breath."

"Wow, I should have expected you to say some sick shit like that."

"So you don't think standing next to a sweaty chick and waiting for her sweat to hit you isn't sick?"

He looked up in the air for a minute.

"Maybe sick but sexy. You my friend are what they call a troubled man."

"I've been told that before."

Fresh and Spazz carried Chino out, who didn't even wake up while they were dragging him out of the door. Wise, Ant, Mu and Kane followed them out the door. I stayed behind and call Sophie. As usual she was blowing up my phone.

"What's up Sophie?"

"Chase why haven't you called me today."

"I was busy."

"Are you coming over tonight?"

"No, I've got some things to take care of."

"What things?"

"Business."

"Are you sure it's business and not another chick."

"Bye Sophie."

"But Chase."

I hung up on her before she could finish.

CHASE
CHAPTER EIGHT

“Hello.” I answered the phone because it wouldn’t stop ringing.

“Chase! I’ve been calling you all night!”

“Who is this?” I still had my eyes closed.

“It’s Sophie! Chase wake up!”

“I’m up, I’m up.”

“Chase, some men approached me last night. They cornered me in front of my building.”

“What they say?” I opened my eyes.

“What they say? How about asking me if I’m ok?

“Well you on the phone with me now so obviously you’re ok. What did they say to you? Their exact words.”

“Tell Chase, it’s that easy.”

“That’s it?”

“Yep and they walked off. What’s going on Chase?”

“Let me call you back.”

“Call me back? I’m scared Chase.”

“I understand that but in order for me to take care of this I have to get off the phone with you.”

“Tell me what’s going on?”

“Later. You want me to handle this or not?”

“What does that mean? How are you going to handle it?”

“I’ll call you back.”

I hung up and looked at the time. It was seven in the morning. I jumped out the bed and threw some sweats and a wife beater on. I called Ant and told him to get everybody to my house ASAP. I woke Wise up and was waiting for him to get dressed. I made sure I didn’t wake up Trisha; it was too early to hear her mouth.

“Ight what’s going on Chase?” Wise asked coming out into the living room.

“Some dudes cornered Sophie last night. They told her to tell me, it’s that easy.”

“They want you to know that they can get to you. Is she ok?” Wise was still putting his shoes on.

“Yea she's good. “

“You about to go over there?”

“For what?”

“To check on your girl Chase.”

“She’s not my girl.”

“That girl has been around you for weeks. Go and check on her.”

“Later, right now I got the guys on their way. I need you to call Mu and Kane and see if they can find out anything.”

"Ok, make sure you tell those fools to keep it down because your aunt is sleep and you don't want her in this. I don't know why you didn't just tell them to go to the spot."

"Because this is easier and closer."

Wise nodded at me and went make his phone calls. Being tested was apart of this business, I was used to it. Whoever it was, they want to see what I'm made of. I have no problem showing them. I could hear the cars pulling up in front of the house simultaneously. They sounded like a bunch of loud gorillas coming into the house.

"Shut the fuck up!" I had to quiet them down before they woke Trisha up.

"What happened?" Ant was the first to speak while everyone else grabbed a seat.

"Somebody has a problem with me."

"What's new?" Ant was being sarcastic.

"Who?" Spazz was at attention.

"Hopefully we find that out soon. Some dudes ran up on Sophie last night, wanted to let me know how easy it is to get to me."

"What? Did they hurt her?" Chino almost jumped up out his chair."

"No Chino, they didn't touch her. She's good."

"

"Ok cool but why aren't you with her?" Chino was very concerned about his friend.

"Because I'm here trying to take care of business."

"Shouldn't Mu and Kane be here to?" Ant was looking around.

"We got them trying to find out who these dudes are."

Wise was just walking back in the room.

"OK so everybody keeps their eyes open. Anybody even look at y'all wrong, snatch them up. Once we hear back from Mu and Kane then I'll let you know what's next." I shook everybody's hands and they were out the door.

Now I had to go deal with Sophie. Once I took a shower and threw some real clothes on I headed out. I had to think this out though. If they feeling like it's that easy to get to me then why not come to me directly? Going after Sophie doesn't effect me, not the way they thinking it would. They want to scare me but not approach me which means they fear me and that means I still have the upper hand. Before going to Sophie's I stopped at Papo's house; I've been watching his house for the past few weeks but this was the first time I came out here during the day. I stayed a good distance away but could still see the front door. Papo didn't live the life that you thought he would live with the type of money he was making. He blended in with the middle class working people which to me was a smart move. I sat there for about an hour then left to go to see Sophie. I didn't know what I was looking for but my gut told me I would find it, eventually. I would just have to be patient.

"Chase, I called you at 7am, it's now 12. What took you so long?"

"I'm here now. You good?"

"No! I'm not good. What the fuck is going on?"

"Somebody wanted to make a point and they thought they could do it by coming to you."

"Are you in trouble Chase?"

"No."

"I don't know what I would do if something happened to you."

"You would get up every morning like you do now and keep it moving."

"No I wouldn't Chase. You mean a lot to me. I know you probably don't want to hear this but I love you."

"Love? I don't know anything about love Sophie and I'm not trying to learn either."

"Chase, don't play. I'm serious."

"I'm serious to. Love is a word that has no meaning for me."

"Maybe right now but you never know in the future. Things change."

"You're naive to think that."

"You don't think about getting married and having kids one day?"

"Hell no! I'm not having kids and marriage is never a thought."

"Chase, as a man you should want to have a family. Have someone to carry on your legacy. A beautiful baby boy..."

"Stop! I'm not having any fucking kids!"

That shit made me jump up and ready to leave.

"Chase! Don't leave. I'm sorry. Please don't leave."

She threw her arms around me and started kissing my neck, she tried to kiss my lips but she wasn't getting the response she wanted. She stopped for a second to look in my eyes. I'm guessing she was looking for some kind of emotion but there was none. When she realized that there was only one way to keep me there she dropped to her knees. She was a smart girl. She knew that there was no way I was going to leave now and we went into her bedroom. She was sleep when we were done; I put my clothes on and was out the door. It wasn't long before she was blowing my phone up again. I laughed at the message she left on my voicemail. "Chase I can't believe you just left without saying goodbye. I feel like your trying to push me away but I'm not going anywhere. I love you." I knew soon it would be time for me to cut her off. I'm going to miss that head game though. My phone was going off again; it was Wise.

"Yea Wise."

"It was some dudes from Ivy Hill, three deep. They hang out at the park. They're there now. How you want to do this?"

"Tell Mu and Kane to stay close and I'll meet you at the back entrance of the park in ten minutes."

Wise was there when I pulled up. .

"What's up? Where's Mu and Kane?"

"What's up? Mu is posted up by those apartments across from the park and Kane is somewhere in the park keeping an eye out on our friends."

"You ready?"

"Whenever you are."

We put our vests, not that I was worried about these dudes but you never know what the next man is thinking. We went in the park from the back, we could see them standing by a bench in the middle of the park surrounded by trees; it was three of them. I told Wise to stay low for a couple of minutes then follow me when the time was right. Their focus was on the wrong thing, drinking when it should have been on the situation that they was about to be in. It was time, my steps were fast but quiet. I moved behind the trees leading up to where they all were. It took me a second to get to them, I was about to ruin their night.

"What's up?" I asked pointing my gun at each one of them.

Reaching for their guns was useless once they realized I wasn't alone. Wise made his presence known by stepping hard in the ground behind them; they all turned around.

"What's up fellas?" Wise smiled.

"So which one of you told passed on the message that it's that easy?"

None of them answered me.

"Why y'all so quiet? Speak up!" Wise started walking back and forth behind them.

Nobody moved or said anything. I needed to get their attention. Wise came to the front and I went to the back. I stood there staring at the back of their heads, trying to decide who I wanted to make an example out of. It was quiet in the park, almost like we were sharing a moment of silence up until I put a bullet in the back of the one standing in the middle and walked back over to Wise.

"Oh shit!" The other two shouted as they jumped back.

"Ok, so now that your one man down. Which one of you feel like talking?"

"We don't know what you're talking about man!" The one to my right spoke up.

"How do you know that he doesn't know?" Wise pointed at his friend.

"I'm just telling you man. You got the wrong dudes!"

He was sweating and shook up; it was obvious he wasn't the one that made the decisions for his crew so I directed my attention to the other one; the one standing to the left of me. He unlike his friends, stared at me eye to eye but stayed silent

"So you're the one that got a problem with me, huh? Well here I am; right in front of you." I walked up close on him.

I could feel the anger coming off of him. He wanted to make his move so bad but he didn't. I respected his anger though. The adrenaline between the both of us was getting too much to handle.

"Do what the fuck you're going to do!" He yelled.

"You ready to die? You came looking for me so you must be."

"Fuck you!"

I smiled at his braveness; it was rare where I was from. It's too bad though, he would have made a good soldier for the team but everything happens for a reason. I ended the stare going between, I put a bullet in his head. He fell back and hit the ground with his eyes open. They say when a person dies with their eyes open it means that they weren't ready but I disagree; he was ready and it was his time. Wise was staring at me, I could feel it and see it from the corner of my eye but I didn't look back. The one guy left standing was shaking by now and looking as if he was about to cry. I began to walk away but only got a few feet away and turned back around. I briefly looked at Wise who was wondering what I was about to do.

"Hey!" I called out to the one guy left.

He turned around slowly with the look of fear on his face.

"Were they your friends?" I asked point to the dead bodies on the ground.

"Yes." He said nervously.

“You should be with them.” I shot him and he landed on the ground right next to his buddies.

I turned back around and walked back to the cars. Wise got there a couple of minutes after I did.

“What?” I asked Wise who was still staring at me like I was crazy.

“Nothing Chase, let’s just get out of here.”

We heard the sirens from a distance. Wise let Kane know all was good and we left.

CHASE
CHAPTER NINE

"Good morning Trisha."

"Good morning Chase."

"Sounds like you got a little bit of an attitude auntie." I smiled at her.

She rolled her eyes at me and started to make herself a cup of coffee.

"You still mad cause I shot at your boyfriend?"

"You're an asshole Chase, a big fucked up asshole!"

I laughed and she walked out. I followed her into the living room and sat down next to her on the couch.

"Trisha?"

"Leave me alone Chase."

"Don't act like that. Me and him squashed it. Where is he at anyway?"

"He left early, said he had some business to take care of. Let me ask you something Chase, Do you really think that Wise is ok with that fact that you shot at him?"

"Why you say that? Did he say he was planning something?"

"Why do you always think someone is plotting against you?"

"Because most of the time someone is."

"But not your family Chase. What you did to Wise was foul but he's not going to go behind your back and do you dirty. He's going to step to you as a man and you know that."

"So let him do that then."

"You're always ready to brawl or to kill. When is your ass going to be ready for some peace?"

She got up and walked into her room. I followed her.

"I know you're trying to block out the bad shit Trisha but do you even remember how I grew up?"

"Do I remember? I was there Chase! For every bit of it and I'm fucking tired!"

"You're tired but your man is just as involved in the bullshit as I am."

"That's where you're wrong. Wise has a soul."

I didn't even respond to that at first. I stayed silent standing in the doorway of her bedroom looking at her.

"So it's dick over family huh?"

"Chase, get the fuck out of my room. I don't want to talk to you anymore."

"What are you trying to prove Trisha?"

"I don't have shit to prove. I did everything I was supposed to do and more."

"If you say so."

"Do you have any regrets about anything Chase?"

"Regrets? No. I stand by every decision I make."

"Sasha used to say the same bullshit to me."

"Trisha I don't want to talk about your dead sister."

"Why? Because you know that you're more like her than you want to admit. In the end she was cold hearted, look what happened to her."

"Yea I remember. I remember the bullet that killed her belonged to me. One of the happiest days of my life."

She got up, walked over to me then pushed me out of her doorway and slammed the door in my face. I felt my anger about to get the best of me so I grabbed my keys and went outside; my phone started ringing as soon as I hit the step. It was Sophie.

"What?!"

"Hello to you to."

"What do you want Sophie?"

"Damn, what's wrong with you?"

"I'm going to ask you one more time. What do you want?"

"When am I going to see you?"

"When I'm ready to see you."

"You haven't been by in a couple of days and I miss you plus there's something I want to talk to you about."

"Oh yea? What's that?"

"Can you please just come over here?"

"When I get a chance Sophie."

"Ok.'

I hung up and called Papo, told him that I needed to talk to him and was on my way. I didn't give him a chance to say yes or no. I wanted to talk to him face to face. Something was off to me and I needed to know for sure.

"What's up Papo?" I said when he opened the door.

"Chase, good to see you. Come in."

"How you been Papo?"

"I can't complain and even if I did, who would care? How are you?"

"I'm good. I just wanted to talk to you about a couple of things."

"Sure, have a seat. What can I do for you?"

"I know you've got your own ears in the street."

"You're correct." Papo nodded.

"Did you hear about what happened?"

"I heard that Sophie was approached by some men that were looking for you. I was sorry to hear about that. I've known Sophie pretty much her entire life, very nice girl."

"Yea. I'm wondering why now though? I've been out here for years now and anybody that knows me knows what I will do to prove a point. So why be stupid enough to come at me?"

"It's not about stupidity Chase. It's about growth. You may have what somebody else wants and just because you think you're the toughest one in the streets these days, it doesn't stop your competition from feeling like they can do better and be better."

"Yea, I know that but to me it just doesn't add up. Someone better than me wouldn't make it so easy for me to find them especially since they would have known what I would do to them once I found them but I guess I could just be over thinking it."

"Yes, that could be the case as well. On a lighter note, how are you and Sophie doing? Chino told me how close you two are getting."

"By whose words? Chino's? No disrespect but he is just as delusional as Sophie is."

Papo laughed and shook his head yes.

"I agree with you. Chino is not the smartest knife in the drawer."

"I'm not calling him stupid. I'm just saying that in this situation he is way off."

"Chino is way off about a lot. Anyway I hope I was some help to you but I have a meeting in a few minutes."

"No problem. Thank you for giving me some of your time."

"Anytime Chase."

"There is one more thing that I wanted to ask you."

"What's that?"

"What's going on with the Cuco situation?"

"Nothing has changed. When it does I will let you know."

"What's going on Papo? Why are you sitting on this?"

"Chase, my decisions are not your concern. You are to do what I say when I say, that's all. Now excuse me."

He sat back in his chair and turned away from me; he gave me his back. My feet wouldn't move for a second. I could feel the anger boiling up; I had to get out of there. I walked out slowly because there was still a part of me that wanted to turn around and bash that motherfuckers head into the table for talking to me like that. I got to my car, started it but sat there. I want to know what Papo is up to. I pulled off and went around the block. I wanted anybody watching to see me leave but I circled back and parked in watching distance. A few minutes later a cab pulled up and out jumps Cali. She went in the house but the cab didn't leave; which meant she's coming out soon. I'm not letting her go, not this time. I knew I didn't have long; I looked around before getting out of my car to make sure no one else was out there. I ran up to the house and slid along the foundation, I walked slowly around to the back, where Papo's office window was. I could hear Cali's Australian accent. I ran back around the house to where the cab driver was and jumped in the back seat. He turned around to my gun in his face.

"Give me your wallet."

"Oh my god please don't hurt me! Take it, Take it!" He threw the wallet at me.

I grabbed his driver's license out of his wallet then looked him straight in the eye.

"Where are you taking her?"

"The airport."

"Listen to me carefully. I'm going to give you instructions on where to take her and I'm going to follow you. If it even looks like your talking to her; I'm going to shoot out the tires, walk over, put a bullet in your head then go to this address on your license and kill everybody in that house. Do you understand?"

"Yes."

"Good. I want you take the shortcut through Branch Brook Park."

"Then what?"

"I'll take care of the rest."

"Please, I just want to go home to my family."

"If you do exactly what I tell you to do then you will. If I even think you're trying to play me, you or your family won't see tomorrow. Are we clear?"

"Yes."

I jumped out of the back seat with the cab driver's license still in my hand. I got back to my car just as fast as I got out of it and waited. Five minutes later she was back in the cab and on route. The cab driver followed my instructions and drove exactly where I told him. I drove fast to pass them and then stopped the car a few feet ahead. The Cab driver had no choice but to stop. I got out and walked towards the back door, by now Cali had figured out what was going on.

"You piece of shit!" She yelled at the cab driver.

I opened the back door and smiled at her.

"Hello Cali."

"What do you want Chase?"

"Come take a ride with me."

"Kill me here."

"Get out of the car Cali, now."

I think she knew that I would have no problem killing her so she got out. I gave the cab driver his wallet back with more money than he had in it before. I kept his driver license and I told him to look at this as a business transaction and if any cops came looking for me I would have to visit his home. I had the cab driver take Cali's bags out of the trunk and put them in mine. I drove in silence and Cali tried to hide her nervousness. She was looking around the car for either a way to get out or something to stab me with.

"Sit still or I'll put a bullet in each one of your legs." I said looking away from the road so she could see the seriousness in my eyes.

"You're going to pay for this," she was whispering.

"What? I didn't hear you." I put my finger under my ear and leaned closer to her.

"Nothing." She turned away and faced the window.

I took her to the apartment. Of course she didn't want to get out of the car so I motivated her. I grabbed her by her neck and pulled her body out half way, she became cooperative and did the rest by herself.

"Cali I will only hurt you if you make me."

She didn't say anything. I pushed her in the direction of the stairs and we went inside.

"Sit down." I pushed her in the direction of the chair at the table.

"No."

"No?"

I was losing my patience with her. I pulled out my gun and put a bullet into the floor right by her foot.

"What is the matter with you?!" She wasn't expecting that.

"Sit down!"

"I'm not sitting on that dirty chair. You people live like pigs!"

"You people?"

"Yes. You people as in all of you that live here."

"No one lives here. It's a meeting spot."

"Well it's disgusting."

"Go into the bedroom."

I used my gun to point to the room behind her. She walked looking back every couple of seconds. She was surprised to see how nice and clean the bedroom was. One of the crack heads from the neighborhood comes by once a week to clean up. She's does a good job so I throw her a few dollars on top of the three bags I give her This apartment used to be Norey's when she first got back to Jersey. She bought a house and gave the apartment to me and Ant to use for the business.

"Take off your clothes."

Cali's eyes almost fell out of her head and she looked at me like I was crazy.

"Girl I don't want you." I laughed.

I opened the drawer and pulled out a pair of sweatpants and a t-shirt and threw it at her."

“What am I supposed to do with this?” She stared at the clothes like she was looking at rags.

“Put it on.”

“Why?”

“Because I want you to; enough with the questions. “

I was done playing with her and I’m sure she could tell from the look on my face.

“Are you going to just stand there?”

“Are you shy Cali?”

She took off her clothes looking me straight in the eyes. She stood there naked when she was done. I noticed what I thought was a tattoo on her leg.

“What’s the tattoo of?”

“It’s not a tattoo.”

“What is it then?” I looked at it again.

“It’s a brand.”

“A brand? You telling me that the men of Miami are branding their chicks, these days? ” I started laughing.

“It’s nothing you would understand.”

“Your man considers you a piece of cattle, that’s not hard to understand.”

“You have a small mind Chase, you only know what surrounds you. You have no idea what happens in other parts of the world.”

"In other parts of the world, stupid women are getting branded."

"Don't speak to me about things you no nothing about."

She finished changing and stood there with her arms crossed.

"What's that accent? I know you're not originally from Miami."

"None of your business."

"Ok Cali, I see you need some time to feel comfortable with me."

"How long do you plan on keeping me here Chase?"

"I don't know. A day, a week, a month, we'll see. Walk!"

I pushed her back into the living room and this time she sat down. I sat in a chair across from her.

"I'm assuming you were on your way back to Miami, correct?"

"Let's cut the idle chit chat Chase. If you think that you keeping me here will make me talk to you, you're mistaken. Don't waste my time or yours, kill me if you're going to."

"You know Cali, you're a pretty woman but you're extremely rude." I got up from the chair and stood up smiling at her.

"You are quite a character." She laughed at me.

"I have questions Cali and right now you're the only one with the answers."

"You're in over your head kid."

"Is that so?"

"If your not going to kill me then just let me go before it gets worse for you."

"I think I'll keep you for a while. Eventually someone will come looking for you."

I heard cars pulling up; I got up and looked out of the window. The whole team was here and by the looks on their faces it didn't look good.

"Back in the room Cali."

"Fine."

"The window is bolted shut. Please don't try anything stupid. I'm not ready to kill you yet."

She slammed the door to the bedroom shut just when everybody was walking in. One by one they came in and I just waited for the bad news.

"What's wrong?" I asked sitting down and lighting my black n mild.

"Tell him." Wise pushed Spazz towards me.

"We got chased by the cops today."

"The train to be exact." Wise said slapping Spazz on the back of the head.

"How did that happen Spazz?" I felt my blood pressure going up.

"We was helping Mu and Kane out with something and got into it with the cops."

"What do you mean by you got into it with the cops, what happened?" I stood up.

"Instead of just running; these dummies got into a shoot out with the cops then crashed into a store. How they still alive I don't know." Wise was explaining it with disgust on his face.

"You've got to be fucking kidding me! What were y'all thinking about?"

"Getting away." Fresh answered.

"Why do I feel like there's more?" I said turning to look at Mu for an explanation.

"Well, I have a few connects at the police department. Spazz and Fresh have been identified; both of them have records so with a description it wasn't hard to pull them up in the system." Mu was shaking his head while explaining it to me and I was getting madder and madder.

"Y'all let the cops see your face! What I want to know is what the fuck were you two doing to get the train on your asses?"

"Another one of our guys got clipped last night. We needed the help." Mu spoke with his head down.

"So now what?" I asked.

"They got to stay off the streets Chase." Wise said just as mad as I was.

"You're talking about going into hiding?" I was furious.

"Chase, I don't want to go into hiding. Fuck that!" Spazz had the nerve to be angry when he was the one that put himself in this situation.

I was so mad I threw my lit black n mild at Spazz. It hit his shirt then fell on the floor.

"I don't give a fuck what you want! This is not the time for a spotlight on us! You two are going to stay here until I'll tell you otherwise."

"Chase, you need us in the streets. If people don't see us they are going to think you're unprotected." Fresh didn't like the idea of hiding either.

"Fresh, do you understand what's happening? You two get caught and it's over! The cops either taking you to one of two places, jail or the morgue. There's no choice." I started pacing.

"So we're supposed to just sit here and do nothing?" Spazz asked.

"You won't be doing nothing. You two are going to keep an eye on our guest."

"What guest?" Ant asked looking at me with one eye brow raised.

"In the bedroom." I pointed.

Ant hesitated, he didn't want to go look. He stood there staring at me for a minute before walking in the direction of the bedroom.

"This can't be good." Wise said walking behind Ant.

Ant slowly opened the door; him and Wise looked in and saw Cali then closed the door back. They both walked back shaking his heads.

"Who's in there?" Fresh asked Ant.

"Cali." Ant gave me one of his "I don't understand you" looks.

"So we're kidnapping now?" Wise sat down at the table rubbing his head.

"It's a means to an end, I got this. Spazz and Fresh get comfortable and welcome to your new home. You two don't leave here for any reason without my consent. Everybody else get the fuck out of here."

Spazz threw himself down on the couch like a big ass kid and Fresh pulled out a bottle of Gin and started drinking. I had Wise and Ant both shaking their heads at me while walking out of the door. Mu and Kane followed behind them. Before I left, I went in the bedroom to tell Cali that she had some babysitters and that she should get comfortable, there was no Miami in her immediate future. On my way out of the bedroom, I needed to tell her one more thing.

"Oh and I would be on my best behavior if I was you Cali. Spazz and Fresh are not as nice as I am." I smiled at her, closed the door then left.

CHASE
CHAPTER TEN

Emmanuel Diaz and Aaron Medina better known as Fresh and Spazz were featured in today's paper as cop killers. The cops they shot that night didn't make it. The train, the vigilante cops put on the streets to stop car thieves by any means necessary, put word on the street that when they find Fresh and Spazz; they're going to kill them. Mu and Kane took the place of Fresh and Spazz on the streets while still holding down their business with the team's help. It's been about a week and Cali is still here, she kept silent. I thought Fresh and definitely Spazz would have intimidated her by now but that hasn't worked. What's interesting is that I haven't heard anything from anybody regarding her disappearance. I did get a strange call from Papo last night though; checking on me to make sure things were ok. My guess is that he's trying to find out without making me suspicious. Too late for that but I had my own plan.

"Ant, call Chino and tell him we're going out for some drinks. Are you still seeing that chick he set you up with?"

"Yea."

"Good, I'm going to call Sophie and tell her to get her girls to come over to the pool hall and meet us."

"Why? Since when you want to hang out with Chino?" Ant knew me and already knew I was up to no good.

"I think me and Chino need to become closer."

"What you up to Chase?"

"Just make the call. Tell him we will be there in half hour."

"Ok." Ant shook his head but made the call.

I called Sophie and told her to get her girls and meet us. She was happy as hell; I could hear the excitement in her voice. By the time we picked up Chino, stopped at the liquor store and got to the pool hall the girls were already there. Sophie ran and hugged me as soon as she saw me. This place had about thirty pool tables but they didn't serve alcohol. Chino didn't waste any time cracking that bottle of Absolute and that's just what I wanted him to do.

"You good Chino?" I smiled at him.

"Yea Chase, I'm great!"

"I'm doing great to." Sophie said smiling and hugging all over me.

I had to play it cool; I wanted Chino to let his guard down. I played the couple role with Sophie and I played the friend role with Chino. Ant knew exactly what I was doing. I would catch him looking at me and shaking his head. About an hour had past and everybody except me and Ant was drunk. One of our rules was to never be drunk in public. That made you weak and enemies always appear at your weakest moment. Chino was about to learn that lesson the hard way.

"I'm going to the bathroom." Sophie whispered in my ear.

"Take your girls with you, I need to talk to Chino."

"Ok baby," She kissed me and pulled her girlfriends in the direction of the bathroom.

"Chino! You did a good job with that Zee situation." I patted him on the back.

"Thanks Chase, I appreciate that."

"Hey Chino, what did you do with that bag of dope that you copped that night?" Ant asked pouring himself a drink.

"Oh, I threw that away."

"Did you tell your pops how good you did?" I asked.

"Nah, he doesn't care." Chino looked down at the floor.

"That's too bad. I know you're trying to impress him but he's being too hard on you."

"What do you mean? Did he say something about to you?"

"It's not my place to share what he said about you Chino. Come on, let's grab a drink."

"I want to know Chase."

"Ok, I guess I owe you that, but first let me ask you this. What kind of relationship do you have with your pops?"

"Honestly, sometimes I think the man hates me."

"Why would a father hate his son?" Ant asked looking sad and was about to feel sorry for Chino.

"I guess I can tell you guys the truth. You're the only friends I have."

Ant gave me one of his bullshit looks again.

"We're listening Chino." I said ignoring Ant.

"My real father used to work for Papo. The way I heard it, they were friends at one point. They grew up together and even started hustling together. My father started getting high and fucking up. We hardly ever saw him though; he was always in the streets. Then one day he stopped coming by all together. Me and my mom moved in with Papo and Leticia when I was seven; Leticia was about six. I was told that her mother died a few years before that. It wasn't long before Papo married my mother. While my mother was alive, everything was good. She died when I was fifteen. Me and Leticia didn't find out she had cancer until she was already gone. My father wouldn't let her tell anybody. When she died, so did his love for me."

"Damn Chino." Ant looked like he was about to cry.

I snapped my fingers in front of Ant's face to snap him out it.

"Yea Ant. I called Papo my father out of respect for my mother but I don't think he ever wanted to be."

"From the way he talks, I think your right." I had to change the mood of this conversation.

"He's talked to you about that Chase?"

"Not in so many words, but he did say that he doesn't trust you because you don't carry his blood. He said he has no use for you and asked me to keep you busy so he doesn't have to deal with you. I sorry that you have to hear this from me but I'm your friend. I'm going to always tell you the truth."

The look on Chino's face was priceless. I looked over at Ant and winked at him. Chino didn't say anything else he just walked over to the bottle of vodka and started taking shots.

"I'm going to the bathroom." Chino said after the sixth shot.

"Don't do this Chase." Ant was staring at me.

"Listen Ant, if you can't handle this then get the fuck out of here."

Ant knew he had no choice; walking away from me now means walking away from the team and he wasn't ready to do that. He shook his head, took two shots and walked over to the pool table. The girls came back from the bathroom and continued drinking. I sat on a stool off to the side, I wanted to be alone with my thoughts. My phone started going off, it was Papo.

"Hello."

"We need to talk. Can you come by tonight?"

"Absolutely." I hung up with a smile on my face.

"Who was that?" Sophie asked taking me out of my zone.

"Nobody."

"Chase was that a girl?"

"What?" I looked at her like she was crazy.

"You heard me. Was that a girl?"

"No Sophie."

"Then why won't you tell me who it was? Let me see your phone."

"You're acting crazy." I walked away from her.

"So I can't see your phone?" She followed me.

"Hell no! Matter of fact, it's time to go."

Chino came back staggering from the bathroom, he was drunk as hell. I paid for everything and started making my way towards the door. Here comes Sophie.

"Wait Chase, I'm sorry. I shouldn't have drank so much." Sophie started pulling at my arm.

"I'll see you later Sophie."

"No Chase, I need to talk to you."

"You were with me all night, you had plenty chance to talk to me."

"I know, I know. Come home with me."

"Negative. I have something to do."

"I know you're going to see a bitch, Chase!"

"And goodnight to you to. Alexandria, get your friend home please. Get home safe." I left.

"Chase!" She was screaming my name for a good five minutes.

Ant was in the passenger seat quiet and Chino was in the back seat passed out. I dropped Ant off first then I drove Chino to Papo's house. He was so drunk he didn't even know he was home. I dragged him out the car and rang the bell. Papo opened the door.

"Chase."

"Papo, I'm sorry I had to bring him home like this. I got a call from the bar saying he was drunk and acting crazy so I picked him up."

"Thank you. Chino!" Papo grabbed Chino and slapped him.

I don't think Chino even felt that, he mumbled a couple of words then put his head back down. I was surprised that he was still standing up.

"You're disgusting! Go to your room!"Papo was furious.

Chino started laughing, when he tried to walk by himself he fell. He crawled up the stairs. It took everything in me not to laugh. Papo rubbed his head and walked into his office, I followed him.

"Have a seat Chase."

"What's going on Papo?"

"Is she dead?"

"Is who dead?"

"Chase, I don't want to play games."

"I don't play games Papo."

"You're a smart kid Chase. You definitely know how to move the product and as an enforcer, there's no one better but never mistake your position. You will never be me."

"Papo, I think you should never mistake my position. I don't need to be you."

"Your arrogance will prove to be your downfall."

"Really? I wonder what yours will be."

"Are you threatening me Chase?"

"No. I have too much respect for you to threaten you Papo. I'm simply saying that everyone has a downfall. You pointed out mines, what will be yours?"

"Ok, you tell me kid. What do you think my downfall will be?"

"Chino."

"Chino? Why would you say that?" He wasn't expecting that answer.

"Papo, I would never say this to anyone else including Chino but we both know he's an embarrassment to you. He's killing your reputation in the streets."

"What have you heard?"

"That judging by your son, you don't have everything under control."

Papo was quiet for a minute. I could see the disappointment in his face.

"I don't know what to do about Chino. I don't want him representing me in the streets but I can't deny that he's my son."

"Step father, right? Chino's real pops worked for you."

"He told you that?" Another response he wasn't accepting.

"Yea he did and." I stopped talking.

"And what?"

"Nothing, he was talking out of anger."

"Say it!"

"He said that once his mother died so did his love for you but like I said he was talking out of anger."

"What did he have to be angry about?"

"I think I've said too much already."

"You haven't said enough Chase."

“Listen you know Chino more than I do. Ask yourself why he’s angry with you. My concern is that his anger is going to get in the way. We both know he’s already reckless.”

“He has no reason to be angry with me. I’ve given him everything; before and after his mother died.”

“Maybe you should be talking to your son about all this. I just wanted you to know that the streets is watching.”

I got up to leave

“Wait! You need to let Cali go Chase.”

“Cali who?”

I walked out. Now all I need to do is wait for that seed that I planted to grow and watch nature takes its course. I headed home. I parked my car and sat outside on the steps. There's a piece missing though. What am I missing? What is Papo trying to do? Why hasn’t someone come looking for Cali yet? Cali has to be the key to all this. I jumped off the steps then got in my car and headed to the apartment. I walked in the apartment and both Fresh and Spazz was passed out. Fresh was on the couch and Spazz was on the floor, I wanted to slap both of them awake after I looked around the room and saw all the empty bottles but instead I stepped over them and walked into the room Cali was in. She was sitting straight up on the bed, focused on the walls in the room.

"What’s up Cali?"

“I still have nothing to say so don't waste your time."

I stared at her in silence wondering what did I miss. I checked out the clothes she had on and the luggage she had in the trunk, beside a couple pair of pants and a few shirts, there was nothing else. There had to be something that I missed.

"What's your problem?" She looked nervous trying to figure out what was going on in my mind.

I still didn't speak and I didn't take my eyes off of her. I looked down at her feet, she had them same boots on since day one. She never takes them off.

"What's wrong with you!" She yelled this time.

I charged at her pushing her down on the bed. I grabbed her legs and held on tight so she couldn't move.

"No!!!!" She tried to fight me.

Her hands balled into fists and she was swinging, hard. I spread her legs apart as far as I could and put my knee straight down the middle. She moaned from the pain."

"Don't move Cali."

For the first time I saw fear in her eyes. I grabbed her right leg and took her boot off. I looked down at her and she was shaking. I grabbed her left leg and took that boot off. I smiled at her, she turned and faced the wall. I lifted my knee up and back off of her. She slowly sat up and looked at me confused, I started to laugh.

"What? You thought I was going to rape you? Pussy is the only thing I won't take." I grabbed her boots off the floor then gave her my back.

The sound of her body moving off of the bed put me on notice which made me react quickly. I turned in time to miss the razor that was inches away from my neck. I grabbed her arm and twisted it until she hit the floor on her knees. I squeezed the hand with the razor in it until I saw blood and heard her scream. I let her hand go and the razor fell, bloody. I left her sitting there holding onto to her cut up hand. I grabbed the boots and started looking through the left one first, nothing. It was the right boot that had something taped on the inside. I pulled out a key. It was small and silver with the letters EWR (Newark International Airport) on it.

"Fuck you!" She screamed.

She slid on the floor back to the bed and stayed there holding her hand which was still dripping with blood. I picked the razor off the floor and went into the bathroom but first I had to step over Spazz and Fresh who was still knocked out. I cracked the bathroom window and tossed the razor out. There was a first aide kit under the sink, I grabbed it with some towels and took it back into the room. Cali was now sitting on the bed. Her body tensed up when I came closer to her. I threw the bottle of peroxide down on the bed and sat down.

"Give me your hand."

"Why?"

“Just give me your fucking hand?” I grabbed her hand and put it on the towel I had folded on my lap.

I opened the bottle of peroxide and soaked her hand with it. She was looking at me like I was crazy.

"Are you kidding me? You want to be nice now? You’re a fool if you don’t think your going to pay for this. You obviously have a death wish.”

"I'll face death like I do everything else Cali, eyes open and with a plan. You know you could save me a trip and tell me everything I'm going to find out in this locker."

She didn’t speak.

“That’s what I thought. “ I tossed the bandages at her then got up and left. Now I needed to get these dumb asses up.

"Yo!"

I kicked the couch that Fresh was on and both of them jumped up. As soon as they saw it was me they tried to straighten up and act like they weren't sleep a few minutes before. Spazz got off the floor and sat on the couch.

“What’s up Chase?” Fresh asked looking like he was still drunk.

I pointed at the door to the room Cali was in.

"You’re supposed to be watching her, so watch her! If you hear anything coming from out of there, go in and be on point!"

I get a nod yes from both of them, I left. It took me ten minutes to get to the airport. I got a cup of coffee and walked around for a few minutes before following the signs to the lockers. I looked at the key and matched the number on it with the number on the locker. I looked around first to make sure everybody was minding their own business then I opened the locker. A small black back pack was in it. I grabbed it, closed the locker and slowly walked back to my car. I drove out of the area first before pulling over to see what was in Cali’s bag. The only thing that was in there was a wallet. I pulled out the picture ID; I had to look at it twice because it didn’t look like Cali at all. Her hair was much longer and blond instead of black. I looked at her name, it read: Calina Ross 110 S. Shore Drive Miami Beach Fl 33141. I grabbed my phone.

“Norey."

"Hey Chase, what's up?"

"I need an address checked out for me but it's in Miami."

"No problem, I have a friend that transferred to the Miami dmv.”

"Good."

I gave Norey the address, and then got off the phone. I wanted to check in with Wise to see what was going on but before I could stop it, I hit the answer button on a call that was coming through. It was Sophie, I took a deep breath.

"Yea Sophie."

"I'm glad you still remember my name."

"You're a funny girl."

"I'm glad you think this is funny Chase, I don't. I need to see you."

"Soon, ok. I'm dealing with some shit right now."

"You're always dealing with some shit. Chase, please. I really need to see you.

"I'll be there when I can Sophie."

"When is that Chase?"

"Listen I'll be over there in a few."

"A few what Chase? A few weeks? A week days? A few hours?"

"A few minutes, I'm on my way."

"Chase?"

"I said a few minutes! I'll see you when I get there."

"Ok."

My plan was to go over there, listen to her talk about her feelings, get some head and get the fuck out of there. My phone started ringing again.

"What?!"

"Chase, its Chino. Can I crash at the apartment tonight? Me and my pops just had a huge fight. He threw me out."

"Come to my house. Fresh and Spazz are still at the apartment. I'll pick you up."

"Thanks Chase."

I hung up, it was coming together nicely.

CHASE
CHAPTER ELEVEN

"License and registration." The cop was standing at my window

"Why did you pull me over officer?" This was the last thing I needed.

"The speed limit is sixty five not seventy five."

"I didn't know I was going that fast."

"I'll repeat myself. License and registration."

I went for the glove compartment and he put his hand on his gun. I slowed down my movements and grabbed the insurance card.

"My license is in my back pocket. Can I reach for it without you shooting me?"

"I would move slowly, if I were you."

I reached for my wallet while this fucking cop took his flashlight and shined it in Sophie's, Chino's and Ant's face.

"Where you guys headed?"

"We're going to the movies officer." Sophie leaned over me to talk to the cop."

I handed him my license.

"Wait right here."

"Nah, I'm going to pull the fuck off as soon as you take your fat ass back to your car." I whispered.

"What did you say?"

I know he couldn't have heard what I said. I didn't say it loud enough.

"Nothing."

He walked back to his car.

"Chase, don't piss him off." Sophie said watching the cop walk away.

"Fuck him; I don't have shit in the car."

"Chase?" Chino cleared his throat.

"What Chino?"

"I'm dirty."

"You're kidding me right? What you got on you Chino?" I was looking at him through the rearview mirror.

"Dope." Chino said putting his head down

"Dope? What the fuck are you doing with dope Chino?" Ant smacked him on the back of the head.

"We don't have time for that right now. Give it to me and do it slow you dumb motherfucker." I wanted to hurt Chino.

I slid my hand slowly behind the seat, low enough so the cop wouldn't be able to see anything. Chino dropped two bags of dope in my hand. I placed the opened hand in front of Sophie.

"What?" She looked confused.

"Hide them."

"No Chase! Hell no! I'll take the wrap for it." Chino jumped up and tried to grab the bags out of my hand but I closed it before he could get a chance.

“Sit back you stupid motherfucker. He would have to call a female officer to come check her. If he does then we worry about it.”

“Chase, how do you know he’s not doing that now?” Ant was looking a little nervous to.

“I’m watching him through the rearview Ant. He’s just checking my information.”

The truth was I didn’t know what that cop was doing. He could have very well been calling a female officer to come and check Sophie but I was hoping for the best.

"The cop is on his way back. What y'all want to do?" I looked at Sophie.

“Oh my God." Chino looked like he was about to throw up.

“Just give it to me." Sophie grabbed the bags out of my hand and stuck them down her pants.”

"Sit back and shut up Chino." I looked at Chino seriously through the rearview.

"Slow down,” was all the cop said before handing me a ticket and my license.

The cop turned around and went back to his car then pulled off. Sophie started breathing again and went to hand the dope back to Chino.

"Nah, don't give him that shit." I put my hand out and she put them in mine.

"I'm sorry Chase." Chino said putting his head down again.

"Yea you are Chino but don't worry I'm going to take care of you."

I could feel Sophie staring me. We skipped the movies and I dropped both him and Ant off.

"So was that a test"? Sophie asked once we got in her apartment.

"Do you feel like it was a test?"

"I feel like you want to see if I'm a down ass chick or not."

"You feel like you are after that, don't you?

"Yea I do, I would do anything for you Chase."

"I don't want you to do anything for me but fuck me when I want some pussy and suck me off when I want some head."

Her eyes opened wide and she immediately started crying.

"Why are you crying?"

"How could you say something like that to me?"

"Sophie, those tears falling from your face is an example of how people can make you weak. I will never allow that."

“You won’t even give us a chance!”

“So it would be better if I put my arms around you and tell you that I love you?”

"Yes!" She screamed as snot started running out of her nose.

"That's why we could never be more than this Sophie. You want me to lie to you. You have no respect for the truth."

“Chase, do you even care about me?”

I took a deep breath. How do I answer that question? If I say no then I'm guaranteed to get no ass but if I say yes then I got to deal with her telling me how much she loves me.

"Don't ask me questions like that Sophie."

"I know you don't love me Chase but do you even care about me? You know what never mind. It doesn't even matter."

"Good, come here." I tried to pull her into my lap.

"No, there's something I need to tell you."

"What?"

"I'm pregnant."

I felt a sharp pain in the stomach, I doubled over. All of a sudden I felt like I couldn't breathe. Sophie was calling my name but I couldn't answer her. I stood up as much as I could and tried to walk towards the door. She ran behind me, pulling at my arm begging me to answer her; I kept moving. When I got to the door she tried to hold on tight. I forced myself to get the door open and pushed my way through it with Sophie still holding on. I had to snatch my arm away from her which caused her to fall backwards and hit the floor. I didn't look back, I kept walking. She stopped calling my name when she realized that she wasn't going to get a response. By the time I got to my car, I was able to stand straight up but I was nauseous. I took a deep breath and tried to get myself together but I felt sick to my stomach. Before I knew it I was bent over, throwing up. I finished and got in my car. I sat there for a second and what Sophie said to me replayed in my head, I punched the dashboard. I started my car and went home.

CHASE
CHAPTER TWELVE

"Chase, Cali's gone." Fresh was on the phone.

"What the fuck do you mean Cali's gone Fresh?!

"I'm sorry."

"I don't want to hear that shit. What happened? What the fuck happened?! You know what don't say anything else. I'm on my way!"

I immediately jumped up.

"Wise!"

"Yea!"

"Let's go, we have to get to the apartment."

"What's going on?"

"Cali’s gone."

"What? What do you mean gone? I knew keeping her wasn’t a good idea Chase."

"I don't want to hear that shit right now!"

"I told you to figure out who these fucking people were before you started playing games with them. Now she's something else we're going to have to worry about."

“Wise, you don’t think I know that shit!”

I called Ant.

"Yea Chase, what's up?"

"You still with Chino?"

"Yea."

"Get over to the apartment."

"What happened?"

"Cali's gone."

"What? Chase, I told you...."

I hung up on him. I felt like my head was about to explode. Wise called Mu and Kane and told them to meet us at the apartment. I drove through lights and stop signs to get there. Surprisingly Wise didn't complain. We ran up the stairs two at a time. I unlocked the door and pushed it open. Both Spazz and Fresh were sitting on the couch looking pitiful.

"What happened?" Wise asked Spazz.

"It was my fault Wise." Fresh raised his hand.

"What the fuck happened?" My teeth were clenched.

"Chase, it wasn't Fresh's fault. I couldn't take it anymore. I had to get some air. I was only gone for a few minutes." Spazz defended his friend.

Fresh got off the couch and walked over to me.

"She said she needed to go to the bathroom. I went in, made sure the window was secure and I closed the door. A second later she screamed, I opened the door and peeked in. She was waiting for me to do that, she slammed the door on me. When I fell, she ran out."

I stared at him like he had lost his mind. Did he just tell me that a girl slammed a door on him and he fell out? I grabbed my gun and hit him in the face with the back of it.

"Chase!" Wise grabbed my arm.

Just then Mu and Kane came through the door. Spazz was helping Fresh off the floor.

"What the fuck is going on?" Kane asked looking at Fresh's face that was bleeding.

"Cali's gone." Wise answered.

"I want you two out in the streets, find Cali!" I pointed at both Fresh and Spazz.

"We're on it Chase." Spazz answered for both of them because Fresh wouldn't even look my direction.

"Hold up Chase. They can't go on the streets. Cops will be all over them." Mu stood in front of the door to stop Fresh and Spazz from leaving.

"Then you and Kane go with them. She hasn't been gone that long so she can't get too far."

"Yea let's go Mu." Kane tapped Mu on the shoulder and all four of them ran out of the apartment.

I sat down on the couch with a headache. My phone kept going off. Every time I looked at it Sophie's name was on the display. I ignored it.

"You ok?" Ant sat down next to me.

"Yea, why you ask?"

"You don't look right."

"I'm good Ant."

I wasn't good. I had to figure a way to get my leverage back. I knew the chances of Fresh and Spazz finding Cali wasn't good at all. There was only one other thing I could do. I jumped off the couch.

"Chino, I want you to drive down to Orange Street and North 7th street. This is who you're looking for." I gave him the picture of Cuco."

"What are we doing Chase?" Wise sounded annoyed.

"We're going to snatch Cuco."

"Why?" Ant was not feeling my plan.

"It's the only way to keep the balance." I was determined.

"I think we should wait and see if Fresh and Spazz find Cali." Wise looked angry.

"No waiting. Ant, go get the van. It's in the back of the building; bring it to the front. Me and Wise will be down there in a minute."

"You sure?" Ant looked nervous for some reason.

"Yea."

I waited until Ant left to turn around to face Wise.

"Listen motherfucker. I don't need you on my neck about every fucking thing I do. My team, my rules. I'm getting tired of telling you that."

"You disrespecting me is not going to get shit back on track. You lack the fundamentals of street knowledge. All you care about is winning and at any cost. I tried to help you but you're too stupid to understand that. The only reason I don't slap the shit out of you is because you're my woman's nephew. You don't have to worry about me looking at you like a son anymore. To me you're just some reckless kid trying to get a name for himself. Let's go get this shit done. Boss!"

Wise pushed past me and walked out of the door. I was ready to kill him but even I knew that wouldn't be a good thing, for now anyway. I followed him outside and we waited in the van until I got the call from Chino then we headed out.

"Do you see Chino?" Ant asked me.

"Yea he's over there parked in front in that Chinese restaurant."

"Who's he talking to?" Wise asked.

"I don't know. He can't know anybody over here."

"He's copping." I watched the dude drop a bag of dope in Chino's hand.

"I'm going to break his fucking neck!" Wise went to jump out the van.

"No! Not now, deal with him later. Right now we're here for something else. Look! There's Cuco. Drive slow Ant."

We put our masks on and got ready. Chino finally noticed us in the van and stood at attention. Ant was trying to get Chino to look behind him since Cuco walked right past him. Chino finally got the picture and ran over to Cuco in an attempt to slow him down. Cuco immediately got suspicious. He turned and looked around and eventually looked at the van. He punched Chino in the face, knocking him down and took off.

"Go Ant!" I screamed.

"Is Chino ok?" Ant asked noticing he was still lying on the ground.

"Fuck him! Get Cuco." I didn't care if Chino was ok or not at this point.

Cuco was running like he was in a marathon. He jumped a fence and ran behind a building.

"Is he going in that building?" Wise asked.

"No, he's cutting through. Ant, go around to 5th street." I knew where he was going.

We got on the block just as Cuco was coming from behind the building. Me and Wise jumped out and chased him. We caught up and tackled him, knocking him to the ground. Ant pulled up and we threw him in the back of the van.

"Ok, Ant let's go." I said jumping back in the van.

"Check on Chino, Chase." Ant was worried..

"Chino!" I called out his name when I heard someone pick up but say nothing.

"Yea." He sounded like he was sleep.

"You good?"

"Yea, I'm good Chase. I'm sorry."

"Just go back to the apartment Chino.

"Ok."

I hung up.

"He's good." I turned to Ant.

When we got back to the apartment Wise snatched Cuco out of the van and forced him up the steps. Chino was just pulling up. When we got inside Ant took Cuco in the bedroom and tied him up to a chair. My phone started ringing.

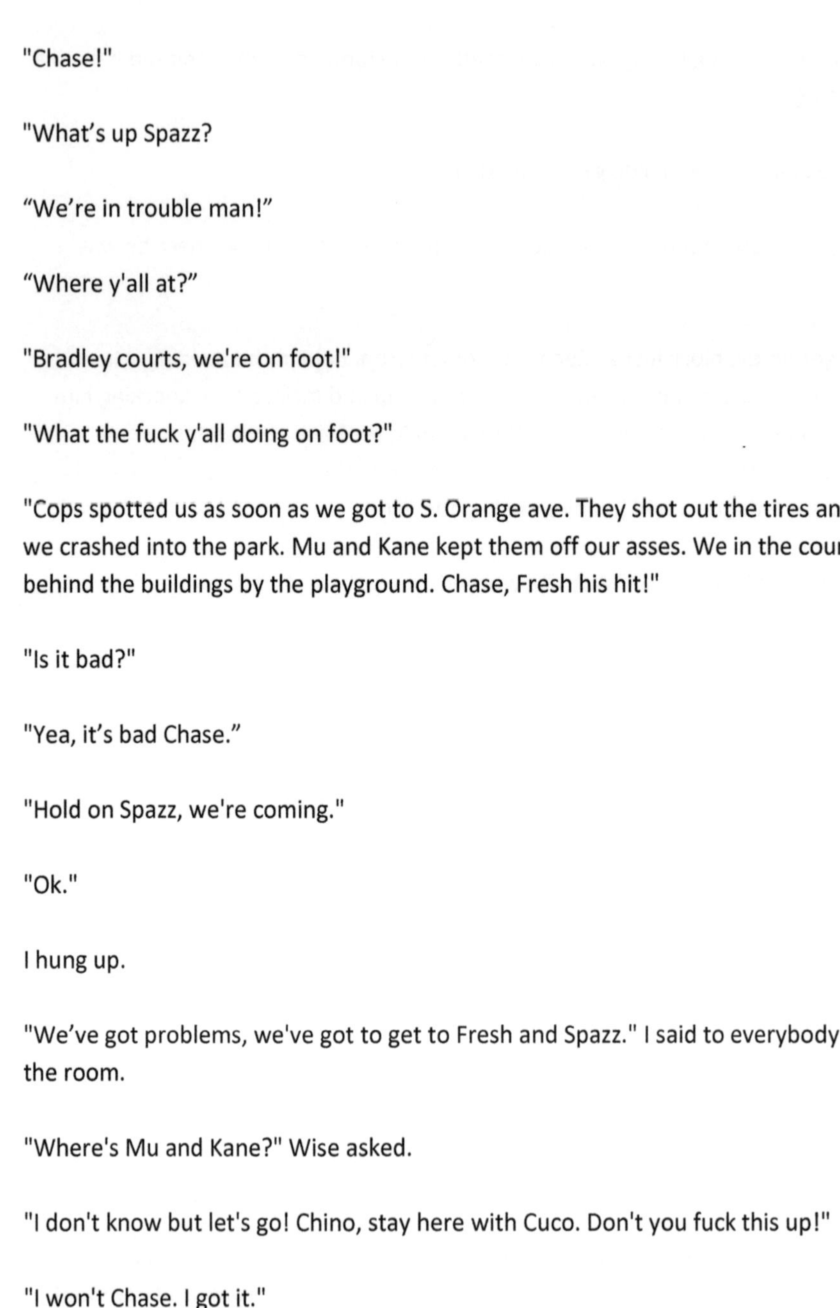

"Chase!"

"What's up Spazz?

“We're in trouble man!”

“Where y'all at?”

"Bradley courts, we're on foot!"

"What the fuck y'all doing on foot?"

"Cops spotted us as soon as we got to S. Orange ave. They shot out the tires and we crashed into the park. Mu and Kane kept them off our asses. We in the courts behind the buildings by the playground. Chase, Fresh his hit!"

"Is it bad?"

"Yea, it's bad Chase.”

"Hold on Spazz, we're coming."

"Ok."

I hung up.

"We've got problems, we've got to get to Fresh and Spazz." I said to everybody in the room.

"Where's Mu and Kane?" Wise asked.

"I don't know but let's go! Chino, stay here with Cuco. Don't you fuck this up!"

"I won't Chase. I got it."

Me, Ant and Wise ran out and jumped in Ant's car. As soon as Ant pulled off Wise's phone started ringing.

"Mu! Where ya'll at? How many cops?" Wise sounded scared for his friend.

"Wise, tell them to get to South Orange and drive past the buildings." I could hear Mu screaming in the phone and I had a plan.

"Mu! Get them to follow you to S. Orange ave, past Bradley Courts."

Wise hung up.

"Are they good?" I asked.

"Hell no! They got two trucks on them!" Wise screamed.

"Ok, Ant drive to the back of Bradley courts. We're going to run in and get Spazz and Fresh out of there. Fresh is hit. Ant your job is to help Spazz with Fresh. Wise, me and you are going to wait for Mu and Kane and get those cops off of them." I got my gun ready.

Ant drove as fast as he could and when we go to the buildings he went around to the back.

"Ya'll ready?" He asked.

"Absolutely." I jumped out of the car first.

Me and Wise put our masks on and Ant ran in the direction of the playground. You could hear the cars coming. Mu and Kane were in a truck similar to the cops but with no crash bar and theirs was white. Mu's truck slid onto South Orange ave making loud screeching noises with the cops on their asses. We ran into the middle of the street and got ready to make a mess. I took out the tires on the front truck; making him crash into a bodega on the corner. Wise hit the second truck making it swerve out of control and crashing into a parked car. We took off running back into the buildings. More cops were coming. Ant had the car ready right at the gate as we were running out.

“Oh shit!” I said when I saw Fresh in the back seat covered in blood.

“How many times did he get hit?” Wise said jumping in the back seat with them.

“Twice, we got to get him to a hospital!” Spazz looked like he was about to cry.

“You know we can’t do that Spazz.” I felt bad for Fresh but taking him to a hospital wasn’t going to happen.

“I’m not going to let him die Chase! Ant drive to a hospital man, drop us off!”

“Drop you off?” Ant looked at me.

“Just drop us off! Chase please.” Spazz was begging.

“Ok, drop them off.” I agreed.

We all knew what that meant but every man gets to choose his own fate. Ant drove to the emergency entrance and Wise got out to help Spazz pull Fresh out of the back seat. As soon as the cops standing in the lobby saw all that they came running out.”

“Wise get your ass back in the car!” I screamed.

Wise and Ant were hesitating like they didn’t want to leave but the cops were getting closer.

“Move Ant!” I had to motivate him to leave.

Wise jumped back in and Ant pulled off. We turned around to look out the back window. Fresh was being put on a gurney and Spazz was surrounded by cops. I turned back around; there was nothing else for me to see.

“Do you think Fresh is going to make it?” Ant was trying to look back while he was driving.

“I hope he does Ant, when all this is done I’m going to check on them but now we’ve got to go find Mu and Kane. They’re not answering the phone. They were on Bergen Street when they called. Ant, turn here.” Wise pointed to the Bergen Street sign.

This was the worst possible situation to be in with everything I was trying to do right now. Things were falling apart. We’re two men down. We drove down to Bergen Street and circled the block a couple of times but no sign of them.

“Ant. Head back.” I was done with looking for them.

“We can’t just leave them out here Chase.” Wise still had hope.

“They not out here Wise. What do you want to do?” In my mind they were already dead.

“Keep riding around Ant, they’ve got to be in the area, somewhere.”

Ant circled again but went down one street further. I could hear the change in Wise’s breathing when we saw Mu’s car crashed on the corner. Wise made Ant stop the car and we all jumped out and ran over to see if Mu and Kane was even in there; the car was empty.

"Either they’re dead or the cops got them Wise. We have to go.” I said looking at Wise

Wise didn’t say anything he got back in the car and looked straight. I could tell he was hurting. We headed back to the apartment.

"Hey, everything ok?" Chino greeted us at the door.

"No. Have you heard from Mu and Kane at all?" Wise asked.

"No, where's Spazz and Fresh."

Ant looked at Chino and shook his head no letting him know that things were bad. Wise's phone started ringing.

"Yea, Norey? Are they alive? Ok, ok. I'll call you back. Thanks Norey." He hung his phone up and took a deep breath.

Me, Ant and Chino waited for Wise to tell us what was going on.

"They're not dead but the cops got Mu and Kane down at county."

"Ok that's good. We can find out their bail tomorrow."

"They won't get a bail Chase."

"Why not?" Ant asked

"We all left Jersey because we had to. Every last one of us was wanted by the cops when we left."

"Why you never told me that?"

"If wasn't something you needed to know at the time Chase."

"So why come back to Jersey Wise, why not stay in Atlanta?" Chino asked.

"We knew we had to leave Jersey so we were prepared. Leaving Atlanta wasn't planned. We had to get out of there fast. Jersey seemed like the best place since we still had connections. All we had to do was stay off the cops radar and we did, up until now."

"So it's safe to say that it's a wrap for them." I said already knowing that it was.

"Yea, pretty much." Wise looked defeated.

“Wise wasn’t Mu a cop in Atlanta? How the hell did he pull that off?” Ant asked.

“Back then they wasn’t cross checking like they do now; all we had to do was change our names.”

“So now we down four." My head was starting to hurt.

My phone was ringing, I didn’t want to answer it.

"Yea," I said putting the phone to my ear.

"Cuco is missing, that was a mistake. Now I have something of yours." She hung up.

"What now?" Wise saw the look on my face.

I didn’t answer him at first because I was trying to wrap my head around what Cali just said.

"Wise call Trisha."

"Why Chase? What's wrong?

"Wise just call her."

I was hoping that it wasn't what I was thinking. Cali can't be that stupid.

"She's not answering Chase! What the fuck is going on?"

"We need to get to the house, I need to make sure. Chino stay here! Guard Cuco with your life!”

Me, Wise and Ant ran back out the door. Wise drove like he already was prepared for the worst.

"Trisha! Trisha!" Wise was the first one in the door.

"Trisha!" I called out running in and out of every room.

She was gone. Wise just stood in the middle of the floor staring at me waiting for me to say something.

"Who has her Chase?"

"Cali."

Wise turned around and punched Trisha's glass cabinet sending into crashing down on the floor into a thousand pieces. Ant fell back into the wall shaking his head. I didn't wait for them to come at me with blame. I walked out of the door.

"Chase!" I could hear Ant calling me.

I went to the one person I knew could help me find Cali.

"What can I do for you Chase?" Papo answered the door.

"Cali has Trisha."

"Cali who? Papo walked in his office and sat down behind his desk with me close behind him.

I could tell by that smirk on his face that he thought he had me backed up into a corner and he was loving it.

"I can't help you Chase. I told you your arrogance would be your downfall."

I didn't say anything else; I turned around and left. I drove to Queens, the only place I could really think. I walked through the graveyard and stood in front of the only tombstones that mattered to me. Chase Saeed and Kisha Davis, my parents. I spent my entire life trying to be better than them. Making sure I didn't make the same mistakes they made but Trisha; she spent her whole life trying to prove that she wasn't like her sisters the whole time getting herself deeper and deeper in the life.

"I know Trisha isn't built for this life but she doesn't understand; I'm doing what I have to do." I was talking to my father.

"Looking for absolution?"

I looked up and Cali was a couple of feet away. I stayed calm.

"If you hurt Trisha in anyway. I'm going to kill you slowly then go to that Miami address and murder anybody that shares your last name or even looks like you."

"I knew that would be your response that's why I've already made provisions to have my family moved. Listen Chase, a war is not what we want."

"Oh really?" I looked at her like she was crazy.

"No, we actually would like to work with you."

"Work with me? Lady, if anything happens to Trisha; I'm going to murder all of Miami starting with you. I promise you that."

"Chase, think before you act. It would benefit you to work with us."

"Why the change of heart Cali? Something must have went wrong; what?"

"We had to cancel the deal that we made with Papo."

"Who is we?""

"My husband and I."

"And who's your husband?"

"Lorenzo Ross, I know you don't know who he is. Our business is based in Miami."

"And the deal you made with Papo?"

"First I need to know, if you will help us."

"Help you? Cali, you probably won't live much longer."

"Chase we haven't harmed Trisha and we have no intentions on doing so. We just needed to get you attention."

"Well you definitely have it now."

"All I want you to do is listen and after that you can decide if you want to kill me."

"Talk fast."

"We were supposed to be Papo's new connection and entrance into Miami. Papo wants to move out of New Jersey, start a new life. We were going to give him that opportunity along with an introduction to some key people in Miami. In turn he would turn over his areas in Essex County."

"So what stopped that?"

"At first it was you. Papo underestimated your power in the streets. With you around, taking over would be difficult."

"So I was in the way."

"Yes. You were. Papo made some attempts to get rid of you but he failed."

"It makes sense, but why are you telling me all this? He must have crossed you to."

"Yes. We didn't anticipate Papo's greed. He made another deal with a competitor of ours. When it was found out, our competitor backed out. You see Chase, we're not like the east coast, war is our last option not our first. As far as Papo knows, our competitor made a better deal with someone else. He has no idea that we know."

"What do you want from me Cali?"

"If Papo is gone then you will be the one the streets looks to for cocaine. We want to be your supplier, we can offer assistance."

"What kind of assistance?"

"Men willing to stand behind you, whenever you need them. Cuco will be your connection to us."

"Who is Cuco to you?"

"He's my brother in law, Lorenzo's brother. Think about my offer Chase. There's a lot of money to be made. Meet me here tomorrow, same time. I'll give you Trisha and you give me Cuco."

"And what if I don't want any part of what you're offering?"

"The exchange will still be made. Like I said Chase, a war is never our first option. It's always business for us, but you should also know that our move into New Jersey will be with or without you. "She turned around to walk away.

"Cali."

She stopped and looked my way.

"There better not be even a scratch on Trisha."

"I understand, I'll see you tomorrow." She left.

CHASE

CHAPTER THIRTEEN

"Why are you here Sophie?" I was standing in my front doorway trying to stay calm.

"Why do you think I'm here Chase? Where you been? Why haven't you been answering my calls? She walked past me and into the house.

"I've been busy." I closed door, took a deep breath and went and sat on the couch.

"You're not going to keep ignoring me Chase."

I didn't say anything.

"Chase!"

"What Sophie?" Keeping calm was getting harder and harder.

"I'm pregnant Chase! You're going to have to acknowledge that sooner or later."

"I told you I wasn't having any kids." I looked at the picture on the table of my mother and father.

"What you told me is irrelevant right now! We are having a baby!"

"What do you want me to do Sophie?" I turned and looked at her.

"I want you to act like you give a shit."

"What if I don't? Then what?"

She started crying and I watched. All I could think about was easing her pain; making sure that she didn't do anything that was going to make either one of our lives even harder than it already was. I knew what needed to be done. I got up and put my arms around her, pulling her close to me.

"Go home Sophie." I whispered in her ear.

"Go home?! What is wrong with you?! Why are you doing this to me?!" She started to get hysterical.

"Calm down, I have something to take care of first, then I'm going to come and get you and we will talk about everything you want to talk about. Ok?

"Chase?"

"Listen, I do care about you Sophie and I promise I'm going to make everything alright. Go home and wait for my call. Give me about an hour."

"Okay."

I walked her to the door and watched her leave. I slammed the door and started pacing. This isn't what I wanted and things weren't going the opposite direction. I punched the wall. My mind was racing, I needed to calm down. I sat on the couch looking at the pictures of my mother and father then I looked at the picture of Trisha. I closed my eyes for a few seconds then got up, put my hoodie over my head and walked out. I pulled my phone out as soon as I got in the car.

"Hello." Cali answered.

"Make sure Papo is there."

"Does that mean we have a deal?"

"Yea, for now." I hung up.

I parked halfway up the block from Sophie's house. From where I sat I could see her moving around in her apartment, the curtains were thin. She was pacing back and forth looking at her phone, finally she sat down. I got out and walked down to her house. I looked around to before walking around the back of her building. I broke the window in the door to get my hand through and unlock it. Once I was inside, I called her.

"Hey!" She sounded happy.

"Come outside."

"Ok"

I made my way into the back hallway, stood in the doorway and waited. A second later I heard her running down the stairs.

"Sophie." I called out to her before she ran out the front door.

"Chase, what are you doing back there?"

I motioned for her to come closer to me and when she did I put my arms around her and pulled her even closer.

"What's wrong Chase?"

"I can't let you have this baby Sophie." I whispered in her ear.

"Is that what you came here to tell me?!"

She tried to pull away from me but it was useless. I wasn't going to let go.

"Stop Sophie."

"Chase I can't believe you! Get off of me!"

She was crying and fighting to get me off of her. I locked my arm in place, keeping her body still. She never saw the knife slide down my sleeve and into my hand but she felt the blade pierce her stomach then the fighting stopped and she was quiet. The look of shock on her face disappeared as I pulled the knife out and stuck it in again making it final.

"Chase." She whispered and closed her eyes.

"I told you I would take care of everything." I kissed her on the forehead and laid her down on the floor.

I put the bloody knife in my pocket and went out the back door. I took a deep breath looking at the blood on my hands while I sat in my car.

"I did what I had to do," I said to myself and I pulled off.

I went back to the house to change and get my mind ready for what was next and that was getting Trisha back. My phone had been going off all night but I didn't look at it until now, it was Wise. I didn't want to answer it but I knew he would keep calling.

"What?" I answered.

"What's going on Chase? Did you find out anything?"

"There's going to be an exchange. Trisha for Cuco, tonight."

"Where Chase?"

"Queens."

"Why Queens?"

"Does it matter Wise?"

"No it doesn't."

"Don't bring Chino. I don't want Papo to see him yet."

"Chino disappeared right after you did. We haven't seen him since. Did Papo have something to do with Trisha being kidnapped?"

"No. Where are you now?"

"I'm at Norey's. I couldn't stay in that house without Trisha."

I gave him the address to the cemetery and told him I would see him there. I was still in the bathroom trying to get Sophie's blood off my hands. I heard the front door open and close then my name being called. It was Chino, I didn't answer.

"Chase! Chase!"

I could hear him walking up the steps and getting closer.

"Chase, I got to tell you something man, it's bad. It's real bad." He was crying.

Chino got to the bathroom doorway and stopped. I continued to wash my hands. I heard him take a breath and I looked at him through the mirror over the sink. He had his head down. I wondered if he noticed the light red color coming from my hands going down into the drain.

"Sophie's mother called me. Sophie was found stabbed to death in her hallway."

I didn't say anything, I kept washing my hands.

"Chase!"

Chino grabbed my shoulder trying to make me turn around but I pulled away.

"Chase, are you listening to me? What the fuck is wrong with you? Did you hear what I just said? Sophie is dead!"

I turned the water off and turned to face him.

"Chase!"

I still didn't speak.

"Chase! What's wrong with you?"

"I know!" I finally yelled.

"You know? What do you mean you know? How the fuck do you know?"

All of a sudden Chino got quiet. I looked to see what he was looking at and it was the knife sticking out of my pocket. I pushed the knife back out of sight and Chino backed up. He started grabbing on his hair like he wanted to pull it out.

"Chase. Chase! No! Chase, you didn't! Please tell me you didn't!"

I knew he already knew the answer to that question so I didn't feel the need to respond.

"She was pregnant Chase!" His voice was crackling and tears started to stream down his face.

"How do you know that?" That got my attention.

"She was my friend Chase! She made me promise not to tell you. How could you do that man! How could you?!"

"She gave me no choice."

"What? Are you listening to yourself? What the fuck are you saying? She was carrying your baby!"

"Shut up! I told her no kids! No fucking kids! I meant that."

"What the fuck am I going to do?" Chino started pacing back and forth still holding onto his head.

"Yea Chino what the fuck are you going to do?" I got close up on him.

He pushed me and I grabbed him up by his shirt.

"It's over! Listen to me Chino! It's over. There's nothing you can do about it. Let it go."

"Let it go?! Let it go?! What kind of man are you?" He pulled away from me.

"I'm the man your father trusts instead of you. You want to stay a part of this crew? That means that you forget about Sophie." I pushed my finger hard into his forehead.

He looked real hard at me for a couple of seconds before running out of the house. I knew Chino; he's going to run straight to his father. I waited a few minutes then headed out the door behind him. Like I thought, I followed him right back to his father's house. I parked away from the house and crept to the back where Papo's office was. I listened to the conversation.

"We need to talk!" Chino screamed at Papo.

"About what? Papo sounded uninterested.

"Chase."

"Not now Chino."

"Did you ever love me?"

"What kind of question is that Chino?"

"Why are you allowing Chase to run things?"

"He is doing what he is told to do."

"That's bullshit! He making his own decisions and I know you're allowing him to!"

"Chino I am the head of this family and I will run it my way."

"I am your son! You never gave me the chances you're giving Chase." Chino started crying.

"This is why you could never take my place! You are weak!"

I heard Papo get up from his chair.

"Chase is not a good person!" Chino yelled.

"A good person? Goodness is not a requirement in this line of business Chino besides you are the one who brought him to me."

"If you don't do something then I will."

"You will do nothing! My business is not your concern!"

"You don't understand!"

"No! I'm getting tired of your bullshit! I don't want to hear about this anymore. Leave! I have work to do!"

"You're a fucking fool! You can't see the devil standing in front of you? He's going to play your ass and there won't be shit you can do about it!"

“Be careful of your words Niño (little boy).”

“You’re not fucking listening to me!”

It sounded like Papo through Chino into the wall.

“You’re a disrespectful little boy. If it wasn’t for the memory of your mother I would cut you loose. Do not make me look at you as an enemy.”

Chino’s sister Leticia must have heard the noise because she came running in.

“Papi no! Let him go. Let him go!”

Everything got quiet; it was time for me to go. I knew where Chino was headed next, he had no where else to go so I beat him there and waited. A couple of hours later, he stumbled through the door looking like shit. He froze when he saw me sitting in the chair.

"Chase, I should have known you would be here." He was drunk.

"And I should have known you would go running to daddy."

"I didn't tell him that you killed my friend so don't worry."

"I'm not a monster Chino. I'm a man that knows what has to be done and one day you’re going to understand that. Your father and I are very much alike."

"That's the first thing that you've said that I agree with. Both of y'all don't give two shits about anyone else but yourselves."

“Chino even though your hating me right now I still want to help you."

"Help me with what? I don't need anybody’s help'"

"Your father wants you gone."

"So! What's new?"

"Listen to me Chino. I'm serious. Your father wants you gone."

"What does that mean?"

"You're not stupid. You know what I'm saying. I'm still your friend Chino."

I looked at the time. I didn't have time to finish this, I had to get to Queens. I told Chino to chill and I would be back. I jumped in my car and was out. When I got to the cemetery Wise and Ant were sitting in the car with Cuco. I walked over to the car and opened the back door.

"Get out." I pulled Cuco get out of the car.

Wise and Ant started to get out to.

"No. Y'all stay here. The less people, the smoother it will go."

"You sure Chase?" Ant asked.

"Yea I'm sure."

They got back in the car and I pushed Cuco through the cemetery until we got close to my mother's and father's graves. Cali, Papo and Trisha were already there. Trisha didn't look right to me but it wasn't because of the situation she was in. It was because she was standing so close to her sister's grave. She just stared at the plot.

"Come here Trisha." I waved to snap her out of her trance and motioned for her to come towards me; I pushed Cuco towards Cali.

Trisha gave Cali an evil look then started walking but before the conversation could start, I heard a familiar voice. I couldn't believe this dumb motherfucker was stumbling towards us. It was Chino.

"What are you doing here Chino?" I asked him

"I wanted to see my popsssss." Chino's words were slurring.

"Are you drunk niño (little boy)?" Papo asked.

"Nope, but I'm high!"

Papo's facial expression changed from pity to disgust.

"What is wrong with you Chino?" Papo's disappointment showed on his face.

"According to you, I'm an embarrassment."

"This is not the time Chino."

"I think this is the perfect time dad!"

"Don't do this Chino." Papo warned him.

"Why!"

"Family business is not for the streets!" Papo was losing it.

"Family business! What family? Where is my mother?! She's dead and I didn't even know she was dying because of your fucked up beliefs!"

"You're going too far Chino."

"Fuck you!"

"Fuck me? You little piece of shit! I've done everything for you!" Papo lost it.

"You did everything but love me!"

"Love you?! look at you! You're pathetic and a fucking coward just like that piece of shit daddy you use to have! He left because he didn't want you and left me with his responsibility! How could I love you?!" There was fury in Papo's eyes.

Chino was silent but his facial expression was screaming. I recognized that look though, it was rage. No one expected Chino to pull a gun on Papo but he did.

"Leave Trisha," I whispered in her ear.

Trisha backed up slowly and disappeared in the dark.

"You have the balls to pull a gun on me?!" Papo wasn't scared at all.

"It's the only way to get your attention! You don't love me and you act like you don't see me!"

"I see you now niño. What are you going to do with that gun? Are you man enough to pull the trigger?"

Papo stepped closer to Chino.

"I am a man!" Chino yelled.

"Oh yea? What makes you a man? What have you ever done for yourself? You're no man, not even with that gun in your hand."

"I will fucking shoot you!" Chino's hand was shaking.

"Look at you; your hands are shaking. You want to shoot me? Make sure you don't miss niño."

Papo got a little closer.

"Back up!" The tears started falling down Chino's face.

I didn't think Chino would be man enough to pull a gun out on Papo and even more I never thought he would be man enough to pull the trigger. The sound of the gun going off surprised Papo and Chino both. The stare between the both of them didn't stop even though Papo was falling slowly to the ground. Chino's face turned pale when he realized he shot his father. Ant must have heard the gun shot because was running towards me with his gun out and ready. I put my hand up for him to slow down and by the time he reached me, he understood why.

"What did I do?" Chino fell to the ground with his father.

"Ant, get Chino out of here." I looked at Ant and motioned for him to pick Chino up.

"Chase, is he dead? What did I do?!" Chino was crying over Papo.

"I'm going to take care of him Chino but I need you to go with Ant, ok?"

"Ok."

"Come on Chino, he's going to be alright." Ant pulled Chino off of Papo

"Ant where's Trisha?"

"Wise took her home."

"Ok, take Chino there. I'll meet you in a few."

"You sure Chase?" Ant looked worried.

"Ant, just go."

By this time Cali and Cuco had backed up quite a bit but didn't leave. They needed to see how it played out. Once I made sure Ant and Chino were gone I pulled my gun out but held it down at my side as I walked closer to Papo. He was coughing, he was starting to choke on his own blood. His eyes were bloodshot. I looked down at him and smiled. This wasn't exactly what I'd planned but it actually turned out better than I expected.

"Remember when you told me my arrogance would be my downfall?" I said standing over him.

He couldn't answer me. I wanted to look him in the eyes so I bent down.

"Do you remember when I told you Chino would be yours?" I put the gun close to his chest and pulled the trigger.

I stood up and looked at Cali who smiled and tapped Cuco's shoulder so they could leave. I walked over to my mother and father's grave and stood there for a minute.

"Things are getting ready to change for me." I said out loud.

I walked out of the cemetery and drove to the apartment. When I got there I prepared myself for what was about to happen inside. I knew they were all waiting for me.

"You ok Trisha?" Was the first thing I asked when I walked through the door.

"No Chase, I'm not ok." She was leaning against the wall with Wise standing next to her.

Chino who was sitting on the couch next to Ant jumped off the couch as soon as I walked in the door.

"How's my father Chase?"

"I'm sorry Chino, he didn't make it'"

It took a few minutes for Chino to understand what I had just said but when he did, his knees buckled on him and he fell to the floor. He started crying. Trisha ran over to him and put her arms around him and rubbed his back.

"Why don't you take him in the bedroom Trisha."

Trisha and Wise was looking at me like I was the devil. She picked Chino up and they went in the back. Ant was pacing back and forth.

"What's wrong with you Ant?"

"So with Papo gone, you're up, huh?" Ant was mad.

"Technically Chino's up." I said.

"Chino's in no shape to run anything and even if he was, nobody would trust him. So you'll just slide right in. That was the plan the whole time, wasn't it?

"Does it matter Ant? It is what it is."

"You really believe that don't you?"

"Yea I do."

"You work alone Chase. Everything you do is for yourself and by yourself. Why even have a team?"

Ant walked out slamming the door. Wise was still standing there, looking at me then finally opened his mouth."

"We're taking Chino home with us."

"That's it?" I was waiting to get a lecture from Wise to.
"What else can I say? You're the boss, right?"

Wise walked to the back where Trisha and Chino was. I left; I decided to get a hotel room for the night.

CHASE
CHAPTER FOURTEEN

I got up early, I couldn't sleep. I checked out of the hotel and headed back home. I was hoping that I could get in, change my clothes and get out without running into anybody. I crept inside the house as quietly as I could. I could hear people talking, it was coming from the kitchen. I was going to ignore it but my gut told me I shouldn't. I walked through the living room and into the pantry by the kitchen. I could hear and see good from where I was at. Trisha and Chino were sitting at the kitchen table.

"Did you hear that?" Chino asked looking around.

"I don't hear anything Chino."

"Ok, I thought I heard something. So what are you saying Trisha? That Chase should get a pass because he had a fucked up child hood? He was able to kill his own aunt at fifteen; he's fucked up in the head."

"No he shouldn't get a pass but you'll never beat him if you don't think like him."

Trisha was siding with the enemy. I took a step forward but stopped, I had to get control of myself, first.

"You didn't hear that?" Chino said looking around again.

"No Chino, what are you hearing?"

"He's hearing me." I stepped out into the light.

Trisha didn't move. Chino looked nauseous.

"Sounds like you two are plotting on something."

"No one is plotting anything. If you heard everything then you know everything I said was truth."

Chino stayed quiet.

"Leave." I told Chino.

Chino didn't hesitate to move. I sat down in the seat he left empty.

"How could you kill that girl Chase? How could you kill your child?"

"So you're siding with Chino now?"

"Chase, who do you think you're talking to? I know you; just like I told Chino. I know what you're capable of."

"I did what I had to do." It didn't make any sense to lie to Trisha. She was right, she did know me.

"Yea and I'm going to do what I have to do."

"What does that mean?"

"Get as far away as I can from you."

Trisha stood up. She picked her cigarettes up from the table and started to walk away. I tried to grab her arm.

"No! It's over Chase. I'm done. I don't want to ever see you again." She walked out of the kitchen leaving me at the table by myself.

Trisha would get over it. She's always barked about walking away but I knew she could never do it; at least it's what I thought. I left the house and went looking for Chino. My phone started ringing, it was Ant.

"What Ant."

"Come to the apartment."

"Why?"

"Me and Wise need to talk to you."

"You and Wise?"

"Just get here."

"Yea, I'll be over there soon."

"Good." Ant hung up.

I pulled up in the driveway of Papo's house. I saw a for sale sign on the lawn. I figured since Papo was dead, there was nothing stopping Chino from coming back here. I knocked on the door instead of ringing the bell. When no one responded I tried opening it, it was unlocked. I walked in; from where I was standing it looked like everything was pretty much packed up. All the pictures was gone, just some of the furniture hadn't been moved yet. I heard someone walking in from the next room. I thought it was Chino but it was Leticia, his sister.

"What are you doing in here?!" she yelled.

"I was looking for Chino. The door was open."

"How dare you come to my father's house? He hasn't been dead two weeks yet and you're already disrespecting his memory."

"Look, I'm sorry for you're…."

"Shut up! I don't want your sympathy. You are the cause of all of this! I knew you would be trouble the first day I saw you. Get out!"

I wasn't expecting that kind of reaction from her but it was cool. I turned around to walk out but stopped to look around the house one last time.

"Get out!" She yelled again.

I smiled and left. When I got to my car, I called Cali.

"Hello."

"Cali."

"Yes."

"This is Chase."

"Chase, anything you need you can go through Cuco. That's why we placed him there for you."

"I don't like that arrangement. Cuco works for me now, not the other way around. If I need anything from you then it's you I'm going to call. You good with that?"

"What can I do for you Chase?"

"It's time for me to move."

"Ok, would you like me to arrange for a realtor to contact you?"

"Yea. I know exactly what house I want."

"Ok, then it should be an easy process. I will contact the realtor and we can get the ball rolling. Is there anything else I can do for you?"

"That's it for now."

"Good then. Goodbye." Cali hung up.

I pulled up to the apartment. I didn't immediately go upstairs; I sat in my car for a few minutes. I already knew what I was in for, more lecturing. I walked in and both Ant and Wise was sitting at the table. The both stood up.

"What's up?" I asked looking at both of them.

"We know you killed that girl Chase." Wise spoke first.

"How could you do something like Chase?" Ant looked disgusted.

"I don't know what Chino told you but...."

"Cut the shit Chase! We know you did it but that's something that you're going to have to deal with. We're out." Wise said.

"Who's we?"

"You took things too far man. I can't be a part of what you're about." Ant said shaking his head.

"Since Mu and Kane are away I'm going to take over their business. Ant and Chino are going to roll with me. I know you probably don't give a shit but In case you're wondering Fresh is going to be ok. Him and Spazz should be out in about five years. When they do get out, they're going to roll with me to." Wise was confident.

"I see you've got it all figured out. Where is Chino by the way?"

"He's somewhere safe, where you can't get to him. You didn't want a team anyway Chase. You just wanted followers." Wise said.

"If you say so. I see you finally got a son Wise. Ant's going to make a good Wise Jr."

"Come on man, that's not necessary." Ant said.

"Ant did you ask Wise what happened to your father?"

Wise had a confused look on his face.

"Chase, leave it alone man."

"No Ant, ask that man what happened to your father?"

It was quiet for a few seconds. Ant was looking at me, I was looking at Wise and Wise was looking at Ant. Wise took a deep breath and walked up to Ant.

"I should have told you a long time ago."

"Told me what?" Ant was finally ready to hear the truth. So was I for that matter.

"That dude wasn't your father. He was Norey's boyfriend at the time. I had found out that he put his hands on your mother. She begged me not to hurt him and I didn't but I made sure that he never saw her again."

"Ok, so what happened to my father?"

Wise didn't say anything at first. He looked nervous for a minute which surprised me, I've never seen him like that. He walked away then walked back.

"When I was about ten my mother died of an overdose, I didn't know who my father was. A woman next door took me in. That was Norey's mother. Norey and I grew up in the same house. It was one time and we were so young but she got pregnant. Her mother took care of you for the most part, Norey was still in school and I was in the street but I always made sure you had what you needed. Time passed, Norey grew up and responsibility for you. I was still in the streets but even heavier now. Shit got crazy and I left to go to Atlanta, Norey followed me. I took care of y'all financially but I couldn't give her what she really wanted so she met somebody else. Dude spent more time with you then I could and Norey didn't want to confuse you. I was mad but there wasn't shit I could do. What I didn't know was that he was putting his hands on her. After that, too much time passed and I thought if I told you who I was that it would change the relationship I already had with you so I left it the way it was.

Ant looked like he had just been hit with a bat. That's definitely some shit I wasn't prepared to hear.

"This whole time you were around me and never thought I would want to know that you were my father!"

"I didn't want our relationship to change Ant."

"Of course it would have had to change! You're my father! I don't believe this shit! Everybody's been lying to me my whole life!"

"Your mother and I did what was best for you."

"Bullshit! You both did what was best for you!" Ant headed for the door.

"Ant, wait!" Wise grabbed Ant by the arm.

"Get the fuck off of me!" Ant walked out of the door.

Wise looked at me then went to run behind him.

"Good luck, Dad." I said before he got to the door.

Wise stopped and turned around.

"You will never know what it's like to be a father Chase. You will never have that bond."

"Looks to me, neither will you. Being a father doesn't make you a better man Wise, it makes you a weaker man and in this line of business there is no room for weakness."

"You hold on to that Chase and good luck to you to."

The door slammed.

"You think I need you! All of you are a bunch of weak bitches! Fuck all y'all! I yelled as loud as I could to an empty room.

My phone started ringing.

"What!" I answered it.

"Hello, this is Jackson Realtors. I'm looking for Chase."

"Speaking."

"I was told that you're looking for a particular property."

"Yes I am."

I gave the realtor all the information she needed and I was in her office signing the papers within the hour. I walked out of there with my keys in my hand. I called Cuco and gave him the address and told him to meet me there.

"How did you get back in here?!" Leticia looked like she was ready to fight when she saw me walk in the house.

"I have the keys." I said smiling at her.

"How did you get keys to my father's house?"

"It's my house now, I just bought it."

Leticia stood there in shock. A look of disgust came over her face and she ran over and tried hitting me. I grabbed her by her arms and held on tight. She got frustrated with trying to get free and spit in my face, I let her go. I wiped my face and I stayed calm.

"You are a disgusting piece of shit!"

"And you're trespassing. Get the fuck out before I call the police."

"You want this house? You can have it but you will still never be my father."

"In the end I'm guessing that your father wanted to be me."

The tears ran down her face as she ran out of the room. I looked around the house and smiled. The first room I went in was Papo's old office. His chair and desk was still there. I sat down and it was comfortable, I spun around in the chair to look out the window when I turned back. Leticia was standing in the doorway with her bags in her hands.

"You are a cold hearted monster and one day you're going to pay for everything that you've done."

"Maybe, but today, I'm a businessman. I'll worry about one day, later." I winked at her.

She held back her tears this time and walked out. I laughed as I heard the front door slam. I looked around the office; it still looked and felt like Papo. I planned on gutting out this whole house.

"Chase!" I heard the front door opening and closing."

"In here Cuco."

"I saw Papo's daughter outside, she looked upset."

"I think she has a problem with me in her father's house. I wonder why?" I laughed again.

"So, what are your plans Chase?" Cuco sat down in the chair in front of me.

"First, we need to clear the air. Our initial meeting wasn't a good one so I need to know where you stand."

"I know what happened was just business Chase, its part of the game. I signed up for it."

"Good. I know your loyalty is to your brother Lorenzo and I'll respect that but let me tell you this. If it ever comes to my attention that you or your brother is not being up front with me. I'll cut your head off and send it back to Miami. Do you understand?"

"Yes." Cuco sat up straight in the chair.

"Ok, on the agenda for today, recruiting. I want a new team, soldiers. Men that have lost all emotion and are ready for war at all times."

"Any particular place you want me to start looking?"

"If you position yourself correctly in the street, then they'll come to you."

"I'll get on it then." Cuco stood up.

"You do that." I turned around to face the window.

Cuco left. In the end, there's no family, friends or even enemies. It's just me and the world in front of me. I'll continue to take what I want and take out anybody in my way. The ones that know me will fear me and the ones that fear me, should.

THE END

CHASE

Lysa Walker

www.ingramcontent.com/pod-product-compliance
Ingram Content Group UK Ltd.
Pitfield, Milton Keynes, MK11 3LW, UK
UKHW041942190726
13854UKWH00004B/1747

9 781304 975782